Conguise Chronicles:

Rise
of the
River Man

(Mutter's Story)

L. S. O'Dea

ISBN-13:978-1-942706-05-2 (LSODea)
ISBN-10:1942706057 (LSODea)

Cover design by Fiona Jayde Media
www.FionaJaydeMedia.com

I love hearing from readers.
Please contact or follow me.

www.LSODea.com

https://www.facebook.com/LSODea_Author

https://twitter.com/lsodea

Or email at lsodea7@gmail.com

If you haven't done so already
GET YOUR FREE
ELECTRONIC COPY OF LAKE OF SINS: SECRETS IN BLOOD
HTTP://LSODEA.COM/DOWNLOAD-SECRETS-IN-BLOOD/

OR GO TO MY WEBSITE: http://www.lsodea.com

If you already have the ebook or prefer physical books (I'm just getting used to reading ebooks myself ☺), you can still signup with my Readers' Group. I sponsor giveaways which often include physical copies of my books and other promotions.

HTTP://LSODEA.COM/JOIN-THE-LAKE-OF-SINS-READERS-GROUP/

To My family:
The older I get, the more I realize how lucky I am to have all of you in my life.

Other Books by L. S. O'Dea

Read more about them on my website:
www.lsodea.com

Lake of Sins Series

Lake Of Sins: Escape (book 1)

Escape is Free in electronic format for a limited time.

Lake Of Sins: Secrets In Blood (book 2)
Lake Of Sins: Hangman's Army (book 3)
Lake Of Sins: Betrayed (book 4)
Lake Of Sins: Whispers From the Past (book 5)

Conguise Chronicles Series

Feeding Fersia

ACKNOWLEDGMENTS

I cannot say this enough. Thank you, thank you, thank you to my beta readers. I am truly grateful to all of you for taking time out of your busy lives to read and talk to me about the story.

Introduction:
The world of the Lake of Sins

This story takes place hundreds of years after the Great Death visited the earth, killing most humans, all domestic animals and all wild animals larger than a turkey. Those who survived were left with the task of rebuilding society.

The new social structure is based on a class system. The classes important to this story are the Almightys, Guards and House Servants.

Almightys, the only direct descendants of the human race, rule the other classes. They are generally between five and six feet tall with pale, alabaster skin.

Guards belong to the Almightys and are used for hunting or protection. They are between four and six feet tall and their hair color varies. Their eyes are usually brown and they have a light coating of hair on their bodies. Most males wear facial hair. They have large canine teeth used for biting and tearing. They are strong, fast and heal quickly. Their senses of hearing, smell and night vision are superior to Almightys.

House Servants also belong to the Almightys but their role in this society is to manage the households and businesses of the Almightys. They are slender in build and between four and five feet tall. They have a light coating of hair covering their bodies. The males are usually clean shaven. They are born with fangs and claws, although their claws are often removed by their masters. Their eyes are usually a vibrant hue and their senses of night vision, hearing and smell are superior to the Guards'.

Unwanted Guards and House Servants are taken to the local shelters and executed if not purchased.

Mutter is a Guard who is no longer wanted. This is his story.

CHAPTER 1

MUTTER WAS IN TROUBLE. No one wanted a Guard like him. He was too big, too strong and too ugly. He stretched out on the concrete floor and winced. His ribs were definitely broken, but he'd fought and won with broken bones in the past. He started coughing. It was this sickness that had cost him the match. He sat up; the coughing subsided. He'd pleaded with Vickers, his Almighty master, not to make him fight but the money had already switched hands. He leaned his head against the bars of the cage. He'd lost the fight and now he'd lose his life.

The door opened and a male Almighty around thirty years old with blond hair entered the room followed by Satcha, the House Servant who ran this establishment. The Guards' Shelter didn't allow visiting at this hour but Almightys did whatever they wanted. Mutter didn't bother to stand up. He'd learned his lesson. Right after he'd arrived, he'd trimmed his beard and had tried to look pleasant, but it had done no good. Every time that he'd run to the front of the cage and had smiled at the

Almightys, he'd smelled the fear on them. Most had tried not to look at him, but he was big and scarred and hard to ignore.

They stopped in front of his cage.

"Ableson, this is the one I told you about," said Satcha. "Looks like he was a fighter. So, he should be used to obeying. I thought he might work for you, but he does have a bad cough."

"Just a little tickle in my throat from this damp, rotten place." He hated Servants. They didn't know when to keep their big mouths shut.

The Almighty remained quiet, his blue eyes never leaving Mutter.

"Come here," said Satcha.

Mutter wanted to stay where he was to annoy the Servant but Guards like him didn't get many chances for a home. He stood slowly, letting the Almighty get used to his size and appearance.

"How old are you?" asked Ableson.

"Not sure. Been around for a while but not too old." That was the safe answer. He had counted nineteen winters but that might be too old or too young. He never could tell what an Almighty wanted.

"By his teeth and body we estimate around twenty-five to thirty years," said Satcha.

Ableson twirled his finger. Mutter understood that signal. Before the fights had started, when the betting happened, he was often sized up by the gamblers. He turned in a circle, giving the Almighty time to study him.

"I'm strong and healthy." That was a lie but he would be healthy again. He just needed a little time and some food.

"I need an obedient Guard." The Almighty's eyes roamed

up and down his frame.

"Won't find one more obedient than me."

"Let's see if that's true." Ableson walked down the aisle. "Is there another Guard who he's close to?"

"Him?" Satcha laughed, following the Almighty. "He's so big and ugly even the other Guards stay away from him."

Ableson stopped in the hallway. "Take this one out."

The Servant opened the cage and slipped a rope over a young Guard's neck. Mutter's chest pinched. Typical. The Almighty's always chose the young ones. His only chance was gone. They would walk out and soon he'd be executed. He started to sit back down, when the three of them stopped in front of his cage.

"Put her in with him," said Ableson.

"Ah, we keep the younger ones separated from the older ones, especially the older males," said Satcha.

The Almighty didn't say a word, but his look was enough. The Servant muttered an apology and opened the door, shoving the young Guard into Mutter's cage.

He glanced at the little Guard who stood as far away from him as possible. She couldn't have been older than nine. She had russet hair and large, frightened, brown eyes.

"Hit her," said Ableson, his tone conversational.

"Wait," said Satcha. "That one's young and attractive. I can find a home for her. Let me get—"

"I'll pay for both." The Almighty's eyes never left Mutter.

Mutter kept his face a mask but his stomach clenched. He didn't want to do this. He'd fought females before but they'd all been experienced fighters.

"I need an obedient Guard," repeated Ableson.

The girl trembled in the corner, tears running down her soft, round cheeks. "Please, don't hurt me."

Pleading never changed anyone's mind. He knew the game and it would be her or him. He stared into the girl's scared brown eyes. "Bruised, broken or dead?"

"Just hit her. I'll tell you when to stop."

Mutter stepped forward. The girl curled in a ball on the floor, pleading and crying. He grabbed her by the shirt. She weighed next to nothing, all skin and bones. He punched her in the gut, making the blow look harder than it was, but the girl was so small she gasped and coughed. He hesitated, waiting for the Almighty to stop this, but no words came. He hit her again. She yelped in pain. He shifted his stance, stalling and praying for the words that would allow him to quit, but the only sounds were the yells of the Guards in the nearby cages. Most screamed for him to stop but some cheered him on. If the Almighty wouldn't end this, he would. His next punch caught her upside the head, knocking her out. He let her slide to the floor.

He walked toward the Almighty.

"I didn't say stop." Ableson's blue eyes challenged him.

He stared at the girl on the floor. Only in the roughest fights, those to the end, did they hit opponents when they were down.

"Forget it. He won't work." Ableson turned and headed for the door.

He'd be dead tomorrow if that Almighty left. The girl's tiny frame was about the size of his arm. She was still breathing. "Wait."

Ableson walked back to the cage. "Obey or I leave. This is

your one warning."

His heart thudded as each footstep moved him closer to the little female. The other Guards had fallen silent. He grasped her by the back of the shirt. Her head lolled to the side, eyes closed. He stared at the tears on her cheeks as he punched her over and over, trying to hit non-vital parts but it was difficult. She was tiny and his fists were big.

"Enough," said the Almighty.

He lowered her to the floor. Her breath was ragged and blood trickled from her lips. His eyes burned, but no wetness came. He hadn't cried since he'd lost his mother. It didn't do any good. He wiped the girl's blood on his shirt as he faced the Almighty.

Ableson smiled at him and handed an envelope to the Servant. "I'll take him."

Satcha looked in the envelope. "Ah, the price for the girl..."

Ableson frowned but handed the Servant a few more bills. Satcha stuck them in his pocket and opened the cage door, putting a rope around Mutter's neck.

"Come." Ableson yanked on the rope.

Mutter fisted his hands, fighting the urge to kill both of them as he stepped out of his cage.

"What about her?" asked Satcha.

"Do what you want with her," said Ableson.

"But...you already paid."

"If she lives, sell her again, or kill her. I don't care." Ableson walked toward the door.

Mutter refused to look back at the girl, the sacrifice for his freedom.

CHAPTER 2

ONCE OUTSIDE, MUTTER CONSIDERED running. The tiny rope around his neck, held by the skinny arm of the Almighty wouldn't stop him, but he wouldn't make it far, not from here. Too much traffic. Too many Almightys and their Guards.

Ableson climbed inside his carriage. "Get in."

He'd never ridden in a carriage. He'd always trailed behind on a chain. He crawled inside. It was small, enclosed like a comfortable cage.

"Sit," said Ableson.

He sat on the bench across from the Almighty. It was soft, smashing up around him.

"I'm Ableson. What do they call you?"

"Mutter."

"That's an odd name."

He shrugged. His older sister had given it to him. She'd hated him, blamed him for losing their home. According to her, before he'd been born she and their mother had lived in a nice home adored by loving Almightys, until their mother had taken up with a stray Guard. As soon as the Almightys had seen Mutter, they'd known his mother had mated with someone besides his sister's father. They'd been planning on sending him and his mother to the Guards' Shelter, but Mom had taken her children and fled. By the time he'd realized that his name was a whisper of hate, he'd had other things to worry about like where he'd find food and shelter. His mother had died when he was five and his sister had abandoned him.

"Do you have anything you want to ask me about your new home or why I picked you?" Ableson's eyes were eager, like he was dying to talk.

"No." He knew better than to question an Almighty. He'd find out everything he needed to know as the days progressed.

Ableson laughed. "The professor is going to love you."

He wasn't quite sure how to respond to that. No one had loved him since his mother.

Ableson stared out the window for several moments. When he turned back toward Mutter his eyes were sad. "I'm sure you wonder why I made you…you know."

He didn't wonder. Almightys were cruel and did as they wanted.

"You have to be curious?"

Obviously the Almighty wanted some kind of response. "You wanted a Guard who would obey. Now, you know. I'll obey."

"That's right. I needed proof that you would do whatever I ask of you."

"I'll do what the Almighty wants." At least until he had the opportunity to run. He'd been a stray before. It wasn't pleasant but he could do it again.

"Excellent." Ableson patted Mutter's leg.

He fought to keep his face impassive when he wanted to punch Ableson over and over again until the memory of the little Guard was gone and all that remained was a bloody piece of Almighty pulp.

"We are working on a very important project. We've failed in the past, but I believe that with you we will succeed. You'll have plenty of good food and a nice place to sleep. I think you'll be happy with me and the professor."

"I'll be happy." He coughed again but this time he had a hard time stopping.

"We'll give you something for that cold." Ableson took out a notepad and began writing.

As the coughing subsided, Mutter relaxed in the comfortable seat. The unconscious face of the battered, little Guard haunted him. He stared out the window, forcing the image away. The night was glorious, warm and sultry. He'd never thought to see the moon again or breathe the fresh air. He'd made the right choice. The little Guard would not have died for him, so why should he have sacrificed himself for her?

The carriage pulled to a stop and they exited. The yard was large with a manicured lawn that stretched to the woods. A red brick, two-story house sat at the end of the driveway next to another larger building which was surrounded by a fence.

"Come, I'll show you where you'll stay." Ableson led him through the fence and into the building.

It was the cleanest place he'd ever seen. The white tile floor was spotless. He shook the dirt off his feet before following Ableson into the building.

They maneuvered through hallways and stairwells,

stopping on the fifth floor. The scent of fear and other smells that he couldn't quite place assailed him.

"Come." Ableson stood in an open doorway.

His instincts told him to run but he'd never find his way back out of the building. He entered the room. It was filled with cages and laboratory equipment.

Ableson unlocked the door to a cage and opened it. "This is your room."

There was a pile of blankets on the floor, more blankets than Mutter had seen in his life and a small table and chair. He swallowed a lump in his throat but entered the cell. He had to sleep somewhere. This wouldn't be permanent. It was probably just for the night.

"I'll bring you some food." Ableson pulled the cage door closed and left.

He leaned down, feeling the blankets. They were soft and smelled like flowers. He wanted collapse into them and sleep until his ribs quit hurting but sounds from the other enclosures drew him forward. He grasped the bars of the cage and inhaled, as deep as he could without causing his cough to start again. He couldn't quite place the scents. The odors of House Servant and Guard were strong but there were other smells too; ones he didn't recognize. There was movement in a few of the cells, but the motion wasn't quite right. In one cage, it was more a dragging than walking and whatever was in the cell next to his, made a noise like claws on the tile, tap, tap, tap as it scurried around its enclosure.

Ableson came back carrying a tray of food. He opened the cage and placed it on the table. Mutter's mouth watered at the selection of meat and bread.

"You can eat in a minute. Take off your shirt," said Ableson.

He pulled his shirt over his head.

Ableson examined his chest, poking and prodding. Mutter tried to keep the pain from showing but the Almighty's fingers seemed to find the exact right spots.

"Give me your arm." Ableson drew blood and then headed for the door. "Enjoy your meal and rest. I'll give you something for the pain tomorrow."

"The pain is almost gone." He couldn't appear weak or sick.

Ableson shook his head. "We are going to work closely together. This will not work if you lie to me."

Mutter lowered his gaze. "I won't. I promise." He could not mess this up. He was caged again and would not be able to flee.

"The pain?"

He raised his eyes but knew better than to hold the Almighty's gaze. It was a sign of disrespect and honestly, he scared most Almightys. "Still hurts but not as bad as before."

"Very good." Ableson pointed to a small door at the back of the cell. "Bathroom is in there. I expect you to stay clean." He left the room, shutting the door behind him.

Mutter waited two seconds and then sat at the table, shoving food into his mouth. It was good. He barely ever got meat and never whole pieces, just scraps. The things in the other cells became more active once Ableson left. He swore a long, skinny, bristly arm shot out from between the bars of the cell next to him. He blinked twice but there was nothing there. It had to be his imagination. It had to be.

CHAPTER 3

THE NEXT MORNING, ABLESON escorted Mutter downstairs. The Almightys in the laboratory ran tests on him and then he was returned to his cell with a meal. The door opened and an older Almighty entered. He was tall and thin with thick, gray hair.

Mutter stopped eating and stood. By Ableson's body language, this was an important Almighty.

"Professor Conguise, this is the Guard I was telling you about," said Ableson.

"He's definitely big, but is he obedient?" The professor's eyes were hard as they roamed up and down Mutter.

"Very," said Ableson.

"The tests?"

"All good. He has a cold and some broken ribs, but nothing that would prevent us from continuing the project."

"Hmm." The professor stared into one of the microscopes on the table and then read the lab reports. He smiled at Ableson. "Let's begin."

Ableson pulled a syringe from a drawer and walked over to the cage. "Give me your arm."

Mutter stepped forward and put his arm through the bars. "What's that?"

"Now, you have a question?" Ableson plunged the needle into Mutter's arm.

"Sorry." The liquid was warm as it flowed into his blood.

"It will help with your cold," said Ableson.

The two Almightys moved to the next cage, so Mutter sat down at the table to finish his breakfast. An arm, thin and hairy stuck through the bars of the neighboring cage. Whatever that thing was, it made him nervous. He was pretty sure that it had spent the night watching him. It didn't move much, but when it did it was fast. Faster than anything he'd ever heard.

"How's he eating?" asked the professor.

"He refuses." Ableson's face paled.

The skinny arm waved in the air, seeming to want whatever they would inject into him.

"Have him moved to the other wing and then feed him."

Ableson nodded, his hand trembling as he marked in his notebook.

They moved on to the next cage, continuing their journey around the room. Sometimes they spoke to the creatures in the cages and sometimes they spoke only to one another. Mutter tried to make out what was in the other enclosures, but they were all situated so that it was impossible to see inside of them. From the scent, he was pretty sure that there were other Guards and House Servants in the cells, but there were other things in here as well, things he couldn't name. Fear trickled down his spine. There was something very wrong about this place. He finished eating and sat on the blankets on the floor, studying the room. He had to become familiar with the routine of this place so he could figure out a way to escape. His eyes drifted shut, but he forced them open. He couldn't let the Almightys think he was sick or weak. They'd take him back to the shelter. He needed to escape not to be sent away to die. His eyes closed again and he shook his head.

The Almightys finished their rounds and stopped in front of his cage.

"He's still awake." Ableson was surprised.

"Stop fighting it," said Conguise. "Lie down. You need to rest."

That was one command he was happy to obey. He collapsed on the blankets and sweet darkness swept over him.

When Mutter awoke, Ableson was at the desk working.

"You're awake. Good." Ableson walked over to the cage.

Mutter stretched and then stilled.

Ableson stopped with his hand on the door. "What is it? Tell me everything, even if it is seems little or unimportant."

"Doesn't hurt." He raised his arms above his head and then swung them back and forth. Not a twinge of pain.

"Really? What about your cough?"

He breathed deeply. No rattle. No tickle. "Gone, I think."

"Fascinating." Ableson went back to his desk, jotted something down in a notebook and then opened the cage door. "Let's go run some tests."

He was starving but he knew better than to mention it. His stomach rumbled as he moved out of the cage.

Ableson laughed as he wrote in his notebook again. "You'll

get breakfast when we get back."

"Breakfast? I just had breakfast."

"That was two days ago."

He followed the Almighty downstairs. It wasn't possible that he'd slept that long. He'd swear that he'd only rested a few minutes but he felt stronger now than ever before. All he'd needed was rest and food. Vickers had made a huge mistake. He could have made the Almighty a fortune.

When they returned from the lab Mutter went back into his cage and Ableson brought more food than he'd seen in his entire life. As he was eating, Conguise entered the room.

"His cold is gone and his ribs are completely mended." Ableson's voice trembled with excitement.

"Not entirely unexpected." Conguise bent, staring into the microscope.

"You never thought—"

"Think about it." The professor straightened. "Guards are known to heal quickly. It is well documented. The serum just enhanced his natural abilities."

"Still, we didn't see this with the others."

Mutter glanced at them, but kept eating. *What others?*

"They weren't injured." The professor studied a few different slides under the microscope. "I agree that this is interesting, but we'll have to run more tests to see how much can be attributed to the serum."

Mutter finished his food and stood, stretching. He was restless. He wanted to move, to run, and to hunt.

The Almightys chatted about the slides and then walked from cage to cage either drawing blood or giving shots. Mutter dropped back onto the blankets but he couldn't relax. The

Almightys finished their rounds and returned to the table, studying the blood that they had drawn.

He could not sit still one more minute. He jumped up and began pacing.

The Almightys stopped working and turned toward him.

"Are you feeling unwell?" asked Ableson.

"I...no." It wasn't smart to ask an Almighty for anything.

"No lies between us. Remember?"

Conguise rolled his eyes and went back to his papers.

Ableson ignored the professor and walked to the cage. "Mutter, tell me what's wrong."

He stopped pacing but kept his eyes averted. "I need to run. I can't sit still." He grasped the bars of the cage. "I'm going crazy in here."

The professor looked up from his work. "Are you normally restless?"

"No, but I used to exercise all the time. I like it here, I do, but"—he began pacing again—"I need to move, run, swim, fight. Anything."

Ableson and the professor shared a glance and then left the room. They stood outside the door whispering. Mutter had no problem hearing every word.

"I don't think it has anything to do with the serum. He was very active in his previous life and we didn't see this with the others," said Ableson.

"But we're taking a more aggressive approach this time," said Conguise.

"I think we should let him out," said Ableson.

"No. Absolutely not. We have too much invested. We need a success."

"We need his trust for this to work," argued Ableson.

"He will obey because his kind was bred to obey."

"I disagree. Yes, they will obey until you are out of sight. We need him to want to obey us. That's the whole point of this isn't it?"

"It's too soon," said the professor, but there was no conviction in his voice.

"Let me take him outside. I'll chain him. He won't run. He won't be able to run."

Mutter held his breath. Some agreement must have been made silently because when the Almightys entered the room, Ableson was smiling. Mutter exhaled softly. He'd won. He'd get to go outside.

"Tonight, I'll take you for a walk"—Ableson's smile fled—"but you have to promise that you'll obey."

He would promise anything for the smallest taste of freedom. "I'll obey."

CHAPTER 4

TO MUTTER IT SEEMED that night would never come, but finally the professor left for the day. Ableson finished cleaning up the office area and walked to the cage, handing Mutter two short chains.

"Put one set around your ankles and one around your wrists."

Mutter stared at the shackles. He wouldn't even be able to stretch his legs.

"I'm sorry but the professor insisted." When Mutter still hesitated, Ableson continued, "It's the only way. I have to know that you won't run before I let you out on your own."

"How can I prove I'll obey if you give me no choice?" Mutter's excitement had vanished.

"It was the best that I could do. We don't have to go."

The thought of not leaving the cell almost sent him into a panic. He attached the chains around his ankles and wrists. At least he'd get fresh air and a different view. It was better than nothing.

"Bend down." Ableson opened the cage. He held a collar and leash in his hands.

This was familiar. Vickers had often made them wear collars before the fights. He bent and the Almighty slipped it around his neck, leaving it loose which was a nice change. Vickers had always tightened it so he could barely breathe.

"Let's go," said Ableson.

Once outside, Ableson waited patiently as Mutter tipped back his head, inhaling deeply. It had rained recently. The odor of damp earth and flowers filled his mind along with the scent of water and rabbits, a lot of rabbits. He yearned to run and hunt. Catch a rabbit and tear into it. He stepped toward the woods, and stumbled, the chains around his feet tethering him.

"Small steps." Ableson gave a slight tug on the leash and Mutter followed.

As they walked around the grounds, Ableson pointed out places of interest—Conguise's home, the Guards' sleeping quarters, the House Servants' quarters, etc. Mutter didn't care, but he grunted every now and then so Ableson thought he was paying attention. He sniffed, focusing on what lived in the forest and crawled over the lawn at dusk and dawn.

Too soon, they headed back to the lab. He almost pleaded for a little more time, but he knew better than to push his luck.

Once inside, Ableson removed the collar and leash. Mutter entered his enclosure, his shoulders drooping.

"Here's the key to the restraints. We'll go again tomorrow. I promise," said Ableson.

He removed the chains. "Thank you." The small gift of breathing the fresh air and feeling the earth under his feet meant more to him than he could express.

"You're welcome." Ableson took the key and left for the evening.

Mutter dropped on the pile of blankets, his large body sizzling with unspent energy.

"How was the outside?" whispered a soft voice.

He sat up. No one but the Almightys had ever spoken to him in here. "Who's asking?"

"Name don't matter no more."

"Where are you?" He moved to the front of his cage. It was a stupid question since he couldn't see inside any of the other enclosures, but the voice didn't seem real. It was so quiet, almost a thought instead of a sound.

"A few down from you, I think. I don't see good anymore but they probably put you where they kept the others like you."

"What others?" This Voice had been here longer than him. This Voice could answer questions. "You tell me what you know about the *others* and this place and I'll tell you about the outside."

"Okay. You first."

Mutter hesitated.

"Please. I've been in here for a long time."

There was desperation in the Voice's tone. Mutter had only been here a few days and he'd been going crazy caged all the time. He went back to his bed, shut his eyes and described the outside, reliving every scent, sound and touch.

"I miss the sky," said the Voice when Mutter finished.

"Ask Ableson. Maybe he'll take you outside." He wanted to pull the words back into his mouth. The Almighty might revoke his walks if the others asked too.

"No. He won't. I've changed too much."

"What do you mean by that?" Cold sweat dripped down his back. There was something not quite right with the sound this creature made.

"They don't think I can speak because they can no longer hear me. I'm glad that you can now," said the Voice.

He moved all over his cage, trying to peer into the other cell. It was impossible. "Are you a Guard?"

"Not exactly. I was a Guard, but now….I'm not sure what I am."

"I don't understand."

"You'll see soon enough. If you want, I'll tell you what I know about the others. The ones who were here before you."

"Yes." He needed to know what had happened to them, especially if they did something that caused them to be sent back to the shelter.

"There were two others while I've been here. There may have been more. They were Guards, like you. They were given shots like you and me. All of us. They changed just like you're changing."

"Changed? I'm not changing."

"You are. We all are. You just don't know it yet."

"I'm fine. I feel great." He pressed his fingers into his ribs. They had healed fast even for a Guard.

"The others did too. They felt strong and hungry. Always, always hungry."

His stomach rumbled. He was eating more now than he'd ever had in his life, but he was still hungry. "What happened to them?"

"They died."

"The Almightys?"

"No. Not how you mean, anyway. The others felt good and then they got sick and died. There was nothing the Almightys could do for them."

"How did they die?"

"In pain, like we all die."

"Sure, but how?" His instincts had warned him from the beginning that there was something not right about this place, but now, they screamed for him to get out, flee before he died.

"They changed but didn't change right. It happens to most of us."

"I'm *not* changing."

The Voice was silent. Mutter sat on the bed. He wasn't different. He was healthy, but he'd been healthy his entire life except for that cold.

"Will you tell me about the outside again tomorrow?"

He was a bit pissed at the Voice. It had promised answers and had given him nothing but worries and questions, still he couldn't deny this small request. "Yes."

The next few weeks fell into a pattern. In the morning his blood was drawn, sometimes he was given a shot. Then he had breakfast. About once a week he was taken to the lab for tests and then there was lunch, dinner and finally his walk.

He was starting to like it here. He had plenty of food and a safe place to sleep. The Almightys hadn't asked him to do anything else he didn't want to do. The only issue was the lack of freedom but Ableson was working on that. The Almighty had already allowed him to stop wearing the wrist restraints. He still wore the ones around his ankles, the collar and leash, but Ableson promised that soon those would also be gone.

He yearned to race through the woods and swim in the canals but he settled for exercising in the cage. He paced and did sit-ups and push-ups, anything to burn the fever in his blood. He'd convinced Ableson to extend the walk to an hour a day. It wasn't enough, but it was better than before. Then, after Ableson returned him to his cell and left, he'd tell his story to the Voice.

That night once he had finished, the Voice said, "I'll be gone in the morning."

The Voice was so faint now that he had to strain to hear it. "You can't die tonight. Ableson is going to take me into the woods tomorrow." It was a lie but if the Voice made it through another night, he'd make up something.

"Mutter, I'm afraid."

He moved to the front of the cell and sat on the floor as close to the other cage as he could get. "Death is peaceful." He didn't know that, but his mother had looked peaceful when she'd died.

"It's not death that I fear. I don't want to be dumped in the sewer."

"You'll be dead. You won't care."

"I'm afraid of the ones who have gone before me."

"They're dead too. Nothing to fear from the dead." Still, a chill ran down his spine.

"I'm not so sure that they were all dead when they were moved."

"What do you mean?"

"The Almightys can't hear well," said the Voice.

"You said that the Guards remove them. We have great hearing. They wouldn't have taken them if they weren't dead."

"There was vibration with some. I felt it through the floor. I think some were...kind of asleep."

"No. You're wrong, the Guards would hear them breathing."

"I don't think so. Some of us can sleep so deep our breathing almost stops. Later, we can awake. I think they used that to escape."

His heart thudded. What the Voice was saying was impossible. "Can you do that?"

"Yes, I think so."

"That's what you're doing tonight?"

"Yes."

"You'll be free. You can see the outside again." He was happy for his friend, but he wanted to go too.

"The others...they were dangerous, like you'll be."

"I'm not changing." But he'd started to wonder. He had loads of energy, more than ever before but that could be due to the consistent, good food. However, a full belly didn't explain how his senses almost hummed with their own life.

"Stop lying to yourself." The Voice was louder, harsh with anger. "You are changing. You are turning into something lethal, something very dangerous."

"I'm dangerous now." He flexed his fists, wanting to hit the Voice until it stopped talking.

"Not like you will be. Not like what might be waiting in the sewer."

"If, and this is a big if, they were alive they'll be long gone by now. The tunnels will lead out to freedom."

"But I'm slow and big and...they might think tasty."

"Then don't go." It was selfish but he didn't want to be

alone in here. The others in the cages didn't talk to him. He was sure that they listened to his stories because there was always movement in the other enclosures as he spoke, but none of them ever said a word.

"I have to. You should too."

"I can't slow my breathing—"

"No. Escape. When you're out at night."

"How? I'm in restraints." The collar and leash wouldn't stop him. Ableson's skinny, little arms wouldn't stop him, but the chains around his legs, those would stop him.

"Break them."

"I can't. I already tried."

"You're stronger now, as you change. Try again."

He hesitated and then grabbed the chains and pulled. His arms ached but nothing. He dropped the shackles on the floor. "See, I'm not stronger. I'm not changing."

"Keep trying. Or find a way. Escape."

He dropped on his bed. "I wish you'd stay." It was the closest he'd come to asking.

"I can't."

He'd expected that answer. Pleading never changed anything.

CHAPTER 5

THE NEXT MORNING, MUTTER stood at the front of his cage as six of the Almightys' Guards drug the body of the thing he'd called the Voice out of the room. It was oblong with no particular shape, just a blob. Two tiny arms stuck out from each side and four tentacles protruded from what was probably its head.

A wet trail on the floor left by the Voice's body ran from the cell out the door. There was no way that thing had ever been a Guard. What else had it lied about? He glanced at the other enclosures. It didn't matter. The Voice had been right about one thing. He needed to get out of here before the things in the other cells got free.

After dinner he paced in his cage. Soon, Ableson would be back for their nightly walk. He had two choices, ask for more freedom or escape with the chains around his ankles. If he escaped, he'd have to hurt Ableson and then the authorities would hunt him down. The streets that the strays inhabited were tough and if he was wanted someone would turn him in for a reward. That left asking for more freedom, but he'd have to be smart in how he worded his request. Unfortunately, he'd never been good with words, only his fists. He dropped on the bed, his mind racing and his muscles twitching with nervous energy.

The door opened and Ableson entered, grumbling under his breath. He sat at the desk.

Mutter walked to the front of the cage.

"I can't take you on a walk tonight. With the"—Ableson's eyes darted to the enclosure where the Voice had lived—"loss, the professor has dumped all the paperwork on me." He smiled, sadly. "I'll make it up to you tomorrow."

Here was his moment. Good or bad, he had to try. "Sir?"

"Yes?" Ableson turned toward him, eyes friendly.

A surge of courage raced through him. "Can I go for the walk alone?" He couldn't stop his legs from bouncing and his hands from clenching at his sides. "Please. I need to smell the air. Run. Swim. Please." If he had to stay locked up, he truly felt that he'd die.

Ableson moved closer to the cage, studying him. Mutter could grab the Almighty, snap his neck and take the keys Ableson kept in his pocket, but he forced himself to remain calm, waiting for the right moment.

"Can I trust you?"

He nodded, hope flaring in his gut.

Ableson glanced at the door. "Give me an hour. I need to make sure that everyone is gone. Then, I'll let you run on your own tonight, but you have to swear that you'll return. I'll get in real trouble if you don't."

"I promise. I'll come back. Thank you. Thank you." He

wanted to drop to his knees and kiss the Almighty's feet.

Ableson's eyes narrowed. "If you run, I will find you and then you'll never leave the cage again."

He swallowed and nodded. Ableson turned and went back to his desk.

The next hour was the longest in his life, but finally Ableson checked the hallway and then came to the cage.

"Put your ankle chain on."

He'd been hoping the Almighty would overlook that, but he bent and did as he was told.

"Be back in thirty minutes." Ableson opened the door.

"Our walk is an hour." He wouldn't get far with these chains on in thirty minutes.

"If you'd rather not go." Ableson started to shut the door.

"No. No, please."

"I'm taking a big risk by doing this." The hardness in Ableson's face softened.

He stepped out of the cage. "Thank you. You don't know how much these walks mean to me." They were the only thing keeping him sane. If he tried to escape and failed, the walks would end. He wasn't sure he could live like that.

"I do understand. I've spoken to the professor about having outside pens too but....well, he doesn't understand what being caged all the time does to you Guards and House Servants." Ableson patted him on the shoulder. "Maybe, the success we have with you will help to convince him to let the others enjoy the outside too."

He cringed inwardly. His escape would eliminate any chance the others had of ever going outside. Still, life was hard. He had to think of himself. "Thank you again."

"Don't let anyone see you," said Ableson.

"I won't." He slipped out the door and hurried down the hallway as fast as his hobbled legs would allow.

Once outside, he headed straight toward the canal that ran near the woods. His scent would be covered by the water. He glanced back at the house and lab; all was quiet. He waded into the ditch, sinking into the cold, dark water. It was refreshing, invigorating. He began to swim, using his chained legs like one big flipper.

He flew through the water, switching from canal to canal but always heading for the city. There he would find something to remove the chain and then he'd lose himself in the strays' alleys. Ableson and Conguise would search the surrounding areas first. It would be weeks before they thought to look in the city. By then, he'd have made a little money and he'd be gone.

CHAPTER 6

MUTTER ARRIVED IN THE city just before dawn. He'd made great time in the water, but he had to find somewhere to hide until he removed the chain. He shuffled through the maze of alleyways. He passed a few stray Guards and Servants but the ones out at this time weren't dangerous. These were the younger ones, the weaker ones, the ones who couldn't fight for the good food at dusk, but instead picked at the leavings. He was in the middle of the city now, a perfect place to hide. The faint smell of meat drew him to the dumpster behind a grocery store. He hid in the shadows and sniffed. There was still some food in the bin, rotten fruit and vegetables. The meat was long gone but they'd toss more. Until then, the fruits and vegetables would have to do.

He glanced around. The area was empty. He moved as quickly as he could to the dumpster, jumping inside and following his nose to the food. He filled his pockets and then hopped out, hobbling into the alley and hiding behind a stack of boxes.

The food was not good, but it stopped the rumble in his stomach. The sunlight had arrived and with it the city came to life. He'd have to wait to find something to remove the chain. He'd search around noon when the city settled down for lunch. He had to have the restraint gone by dusk or risk being attacked. He rested his head against the brick wall and dozed.

A slamming door woke him. A small, female House Servant carried bags from the grocer and tossed them into the dumpster. He inhaled, catching the scent from the bags. *Cleaning supplies, no food.* She paused, her light green eyes scanning the alley. He held his breath, afraid to make the slightest sound. The boxes blocked him from view, but Servants had excellent hearing. Her nostrils quivered and her ears tipped toward him. There was nothing he could do to cover his scent and he'd never reach her before she escaped into the store. All he could do was wait. After a few minutes, she turned and went back inside. A stray Guard around here shouldn't be anything she hadn't encountered before and yet, the alley was quiet. There would be food here every night. Someone should have set up camp like he had. His nerves hummed. Chain or no chain, it was time to go.

He moved up and down the alleyways, searching through the piles of debris for something that he could use to remove the restraint but there was nothing. It was late afternoon when he found himself back at the grocer's. There were no new scents of Almightys or Guards. She hadn't called the authorities about a stray. He stared at the chain. The Voice had said to use his hands to break them. Of course, the Voice wasn't in his right mind or his right body. Still, he sat down, clasping the chain near his ankles and pulled. Nothing. He was not changing. The

Voice had been wrong. He leaned his head against the wall. That left him with only one option.

He made his way toward Sovee's home. It was risky. Sovee belonged to Vickers and could report him, but the older Guard might help him, if the price were right.

He went around the back of the house and tapped at the door. "Sovee, you there? It's me, Mutter." The door opened. Sovee was a big Guard almost as big as him.

Sovee smiled, the scar across his face pulling his one eye almost shut. "I figured you'd be dead by now."

The older Guard stepped back and Mutter slipped inside.

"Someone bought me. Can you believe it?"

"And you repaid them by running?" Sovee stared at Mutter's feet.

"It wasn't a good place."

"We do as we're told." Sovee was a perfect Almighty's Guard, never questioning only obeying. "I tried to teach you that, but"—he shook his head—"you must have been on your own too long."

"Can you help me or not?" He didn't need a lecture.

Sovee nodded and Mutter followed him farther into the house. He'd been here many times over the years. Sovee, who was retired from the ring, trained Vickers' fighters. The old Guard opened a closet and pulled out a pair of bolt cutters.

"Where'd you get those?" Guards were not allowed to have dangerous tools.

Sovee's hard, brown eyes glared at him.

"Sorry. None of my business." As long as the chain was gone, he didn't care what the old Guard did.

Sovee grunted in agreement and with one quick cut the

chain was separated. It took a little more work to remove it from Mutter's ankles but soon he was free.

"Thanks." He headed toward the door.

"Be at the carriage docks tonight when the moon is high."

He should have known he wouldn't get away without paying. "I need money. Do I at least get a cut?"

"I just gave you three." Sovee chuckled at his joke.

He wanted to punch the other Guard in the face, but instead said, "I'm hungry. I need to eat before the fight."

"Then you better hurry. The dumpsters will be picked clean soon, if they aren't already."

Typical. Sovee was no one's friend. He opened the door. The sky was dark. He strode down the alleyways, no longer concerned about the others who lurked in his path. He was big and scarred; there weren't many who would pick a fight with him now that the chain was gone.

When he arrived at the grocer's, the dumpster was empty. There was still a little rotten fruit, but he needed meat. There were lights on in some of the neighboring stores, but the grocer's was dark and quiet. He crept to the building and tried the back door. It was locked. If he broke in, he'd have to find another place to eat tomorrow, but he couldn't fight without food. He glanced around. The alley was empty. He grabbed the handle, shoving his shoulder against the door. It groaned a bit at the pressure and then popped open. He slipped inside and followed his nose to the meat.

There were rows of packages, red, bloody and delicious in the refrigerated section. His mouth watered. He grabbed a handful and turned to leave. A pair of pale green eyes stared at him through the darkness. It was the Servant from earlier. He'd assumed that she'd left with the grocer. He should have been more careful. There was no way he was going back to the shelter especially under these circumstances. The authorities killed thieves right away.

"I don't want any trouble," he said.

"Then you shouldn't have broken into my home." She glided through the shadows.

He kept her in sight as he made his way toward the door. He could kill her with a snap of his wrist, but he'd have to catch her first and that might take time which he didn't have. Plus, she wouldn't go quietly and that would bring help from one of the neighboring stores.

"Put it back and I won't report you."

"I can't do that." He needed this food more than the grocer.

"Then you'll be dead at the shelter tomorrow."

"They'll have to find me first."

"Oh, they'll catch you." She moved out of the shadows, closer to him but still out of reach. "You do not exactly blend in." She was even smaller up close. "Put the meat back and leave." Her voice was firm.

He sniffed. "Why aren't you afraid of me?"

"Why would I be?"

This was a first. All females feared him. Even before his scars he had not been an attractive Guard, his features blunt and hard.

"Just because you're ugly doesn't make you mean or fast and you'll have to be quick to catch me."

She raced forward. Her claws connected with his arm and sliced through his shirt. He lunged for her, ignoring the pain.

He didn't expect to catch her, just scare her away from the door, but his hand locked on her wrist. He spun her around, pulling her flush against him, the packages falling to the floor. He wrapped his other hand around her throat. It would be a simple task to snap her neck, barely a movement, but he hesitated. Her bones, tiny beneath his touch, reminded him of the little Guard. She struggled in his grasp. He blocked every move she made, keeping her close. Her body was firm, yet soft. After a few moments she stilled, her eyes meeting his and holding.

"Now, what?" she asked.

"I don't know." It was obvious that he wasn't going to kill her or he'd have done it by now.

"You can't have the meat. I'll get in trouble."

"You protect this place?" It was a job usually given to Guards or maybe a Guard and Servant, but never a Servant so young and small.

"Yes." The word was almost a hiss. "I'm deadly."

He grinned. "I'm sorry. You're just so little."

"Let me go and I'll show you." She bared her teeth.

He couldn't refuse the dare. He dropped his arms and she attacked. The first slash, across his cheek, caught him by surprise. He'd been sure that she'd run. The second one he blocked, clasping her hand in his and spinning her around, her back tight against his front.

"How did you do that?" She turned her head, trying to see his face. "Guards are not that fast. Ever."

He lowered his lip to her ear. "I am." He'd never been attracted to a Servant, disliked all he'd ever met, before her. She had spirit and it had been a long time since he'd been with a female. Eat then mate, those desires coursed through his blood, demanding.

A bell sounded. She stiffened in his arms. He covered her mouth with his hand to quiet her scream, but she remained silent.

"I forgot my house keys," yelled the grocer. "Help me find them."

"Please leave," she whispered against his palm.

He let her go and hurried out the door. He slipped into the alley, lingering in the shadows. The lights came on in the store and there were voices and movement but nothing to hint that she'd told the Almighty about him. His stomach clenched. He still needed food. Maybe, he could find some on the way to the docks. The lights at the grocery store went out. The back door opened.

She stepped outside, carrying a small bag. She stopped at the dumpster. "Guard," she whispered. "I know you're here. I can smell you." She stuffed the bag under the dumpster. "For you." She went back inside.

He waited a few moments and then darted behind the garbage can and reached underneath. It was a small chunk of meat, barely a bite, but his hand trembled as he put it in his mouth. No one had shown him kindness since his mother. He went back to his spot in the alley. His stomach rumbled more insistently now that it had tasted what it desired. He leaned against the wall, watching the building and waiting for the time to leave.

CHAPTER 7

MUTTER DIDN'T HAVE ANY trouble finding the location of the fight. He'd been here before but only to watch. Vickers' Guards weren't allowed to participate in street fights.

Sovee waved to him. He pushed through the crowd.

"When do I fight?" He wanted to get this done.

"Turn around. Let Noodles take a look at you," said Sovee.

He turned slowly. The betting was starting. He'd fight soon.

"Hmm. You still sick?" asked Noodles.

He faced the other Guards again. "No."

"You were a good fighter. Surprised Vickers let you go," said Noodles.

"I lost."

"You won't lose tonight though, will you?" asked Noodles, his tone hard.

"Nope." He'd like to ask who he was fighting but he needed to be confident. If Sovee didn't make enough money the other Guard might make him fight for free again.

"I'll back him," said Noodles.

"What? Wait." His eyes met Sovee's. "I thought you were backing me." This was not good. He knew Noodles by reputation and if he lost the fight, the other Guard would own him for a long time. He'd be sent on jobs that no one wanted to take like stealing young Guards for the sex trade or catching Servants for the meat market.

"How does me spending my money cancel your debt to me?" Sovee laughed. "Nope. Noodles will back you and I'll bet on you. We all win."

He glared at Sovee. They had never been friends but this was betrayal.

"I don't think he's happy about this." Noodles patted Mutter on the back. "You're up. Go make me some money."

He sent one last glare at Sovee and stepped into the circle in the center of the crowd. His opponent pushed through from the other side. Mutter kept his face impassive. Half the battle was won on perception. If he showed weakness he was done, but this would not be easy. The other Guard was tall and lean with long arms and huge fists.

His opponent approached. By the roar of the crowd the other Guard was moving fast, but to him it was like slow motion. He stepped aside, putting his foot out and tripping his enemy. The Guard hit the ground but jumped up quickly, lashing out and connecting one of his huge paws with Mutter's jaw. He staggered backward, his head spinning but instead of sinking into the dizziness he lunged forward, his fist slamming into the other Guard's chest. The crowd shouted as his opponent landed a few hard blows to Mutter's face and stomach. He felt nothing but the desire to attack. He sent an upper cut to his opponent's jaw and the other Guard stumbled. Mutter wrapped one arm around his enemy as his other fist continued to punch, digging into flesh, over and over. The thuds became a pattern, a chant in his head, kill, kill, kill.

Hands pulled at his shoulders, too many hands. He dropped his hold on the Guard, spun around and attacked. His arms and teeth connected and tore into flesh. Loud voices, some screaming, penetrated his haze. The hands were gone. The crowd had backed away.

The scent of terror was everywhere. The surrounding Guards stared at him, faces pale and eyes wide. He couldn't fight them all. He had to get away. He bared his teeth and stepped backward. His foot hit something soft but solid. His opponent's chest was split open, exposing his organs. Flesh. Meat. He shoved aside his hunger; the silence of the crowd told him he needed to flee now before they organized. He stepped over the body and the crowd parted for him. As soon as he was far enough away he turned and ran.

It wasn't a conscious decision to go back to the grocer's but that was where his feet led him. He stood in the shadows of the alley. He couldn't stay. They would want retribution for what he'd done. He had to find food and then leave. He crept over to the dumpster, knowing there was nothing there but hoping for a crumb.

The door to the shop opened. "There you are. I've been looking for you." The Servant stepped outside, holding a small sack.

"Stay away." His hands trembled at his sides.

"You need to eat something. The little bit of meat that I gave you couldn't have been enough." She continued toward him.

He couldn't let her get close. He might hurt her. He stepped toward the alley, moving out from behind the dumpster.

Her eyes widened, but not in fear. "Holy Araldo, what happened to you?"

The concern in her voice held his feet as she approached.

"Where are you hurt?" Her hands touched his face and arms.

"Not my blood." His head throbbed now, probably from hunger.

"You're burning up. Come with me." She grabbed his hand, hers tiny and soft in his big paw.

He let her lead him into the building. He shouldn't. She could get in trouble for helping him but he followed her into a back room with a sink, pallet of blankets and shelves filled with food.

"I saved this for you." She handed him the bag.

When he opened it, the sharp smell of meat a little past its prime assaulted his nose and his stomach grumbled. He shoved a chunk in his mouth. "Thanks."

She filled a mop bucket with water from the sink. "What happened to you?"

He hesitated, a hunk of meat in his hand. If he told her the truth she'd make him leave. No one had been kind to him in years. He didn't want to lose this, but it was for the best. He stuffed the food into his mouth. "I killed a Guard."

"Were you attacked?" She didn't blink as she stared at him, waiting for the answer.

"No. It was a street fight."

"To the death?"

"No." Her green eyes hardened. He didn't owe her an explanation but he couldn't stop the words. "I didn't mean to do it." He started to pace. "I don't remember doing it. All I remember is hitting him." *Again and again*.

"Do you fight often?" She continued to stare at him, but her eyes were pale green and soft once again.

He stopped pacing. "I used to. I may have to again."

"Did you ever kill anyone before?"

He shook his head. *Except the little girl.* He forced that thought away. That didn't count. He'd had to do that to survive.

"Take off your clothes." She carried the bucket over to him.

His heart skipped a beat and then picked up pace, racing in his chest. His hunger satisfied, his eyes roamed her body. "How old are you?" He wasn't sure if it mattered. His head still pounded and his body was hot, but he'd mate. He'd fought and won. He'd eaten. Now, it was time to mate.

"Not for that reason, you idiot. You reek of blood. They'll follow your trail. "

"You can't be involved in this." He headed for the door.

She grabbed his arm. "I'll take care of it."

"Why?" No one helped anyone without a reason.

She pushed his shirt upward, her hands cool on his hot skin. Suddenly, he was exhausted. His legs trembled. He needed to sleep, now. He wouldn't make it far until he rested, which left him with no choice but to trust her. He lifted his arms and ducked as she pulled his shirt over his head.

Her hands moved to his pants; he pushed them away.

"Turn around." If they weren't going to mate, he didn't want her to see him. He was large and scarred. She'd be frightened.

She smiled but did as he said. He took off his pants and then moved behind a shelf.

"Wash up and then rest. I'll be back soon." She grabbed the clothes from the floor.

He waited several minutes to ensure that she was gone before washing the blood from his face and body. He searched for something to wear, but settled on wrapping a blanket around himself. He would have to sneak out and find new clothes, but right now he needed to sleep before he passed out. He lay on the floor next to the pallet of blankets. He would not touch her bed.

CHAPTER 8

IT WAS DARK WHEN Mutter awoke. He was on the pallet. She was curled up next to him. He was hungry again but the warmth of her body was calling to him. He touched her shoulder and she rolled over, her green eyes hazy with sleep.

"You're awake!" She sat up, touching his cheeks and forehead. "Your fever's gone." She started to stand.

He grabbed her arm, halting her.

"I have some food saved for you." She smiled at him.

He slowly opened his hand, letting her go. She wasn't for him anyway. She was too young. "I ate it all last night."

"No. You've been sleeping for days."

He sat up. "That's impossible." The night before was so fresh in his mind. He could still feel his fists slamming into the other Guard's flesh.

She dropped a bag on his lap and sat next to him while he ate. Once he started he couldn't quit. He was ravenous, but there was only a little meat and he didn't want bread or fruit. He dug through the bag.

"Sorry. I had to toss a lot of the meat after a couple of days. Today, there wasn't much that I was supposed to throw away."

He ate some bread, the crust dry and tasteless in his mouth. "Thanks. This is great."

She gave him a look that said she knew he was lying. "I'll have more tomorrow. There's quite a bit of older meat that the grocer will want me to toss."

He leaned against the wall. He felt good now, better than good. His eyes wandered over her tiny frame. "I need to leave."

"Why?" She tried to hide the hurt in her voice, but failed.

"It's dangerous for you if I stay."

"It's fine. No one is looking this way for you. They did the first day. Followed your trail here, but I did a good job of leading them away." She laughed a little. "I left your clothes at the Lake of Sins. No one will hunt for you there."

"Why are you helping me?"

She scooted closer, her knee brushing against his thigh. "Why didn't you kill me?"

"I don't know." It was the truth. Maybe it was because she wasn't afraid of him or maybe she reminded him too much of the little Guard.

"Why did you kill the Guard?"

"Why do you care, Servant? One less Guard around should be cause for celebrating." He wasn't going to talk about the fight. He started to stand and then realized that he was still naked. He tugged on the blanket but she didn't budge.

"Answer my question." She wrapped the cloth around her hand.

He tugged again, harder. She raised a brow, keeping her hold on the cloth. He had two choices, lose the blanket or settle back down on the pallet next to her. He sat back down.

"I didn't mean to kill him. I...I didn't even know that I had until it was over."

"You are a good Guard." She touched his cheek.

"You know nothing about me." He turned his face away. He'd always done whatever he needed to in order to survive. That did not make him a good anything.

"You didn't kill me and—"

"That's not a good enough reason to risk your life for me. I answered your questions. Now, you answer mine. Why are you helping me?"

She stared at him for a long moment and then sighed. "I don't know. Not really. At first, I was just going to give you the food as a thank you for...well, for not killing me." She smiled.

His heart skipped a beat. She was so young and innocent and he was so hardened and ugly.

"But then when I saw all the blood...I felt bad for you. Life on the street is hard."

He could stand fear and hatred but not pity. He yanked on the blanket, but she held tight.

"I'm leaving. Either give me the blanket or get an eyeful." He shifted to stand.

"I hate being alone. You need somewhere to stay and I...well, I need someone to talk to, live with." A blush crept up her cheeks as she glanced at him from under her lashes.

He didn't know what to say. He'd been alone most of his life, but sometimes he still missed those first few years with his mother.

"Please stay, at least until you're better. The grocer doesn't come back here, so you'll be safe. It's better than living on the street. Right?"

She was pleading. He should tell her that it never worked, but instead he nodded.

She put her hand on his chest and guided him down. She curled up next to him. "What's your name?"

"Mutter." His arm naturally went around her and she snuggled closer.

"Almost like mother," she said.

"No, like mutt. My sister gave me the name. She hated me."

"What did your mother call you?"

"My son. Not really a name I could use, so I kept Mutter." He wasn't sure why he paused. She had eyes; she knew he was ugly. "It fits. I don't exactly look like the others. More of a mix of things."

She leaned up, her hand on his chest. "A good mix. Strong." She ran her finger over his nose and cheek. "Your eyes are so dark brown they're almost black."

He looked away. Soulless most called them. "Scary, I know."

She leaned closer, resting her elbows on his chest and pulled his face back toward hers. "Not scary. Warm and dark like the night. I love the night."

Her lips were close. If he leaned forward just a little he'd be kissing her. "I should leave."

"You're safe here. I promise." Her fingers explored his face, finding each scar and examining it. Her eyes showed nothing but sympathy.

It was as if she healed them with her touch. He was no longer ashamed of how he looked. If she didn't mind, why should he. "What's your name?"

Hurt flickered in her gaze. "I don't have one. Not any longer." She lay back down, still near him but it wasn't the same.

"I'm sorry. I didn't mean to upset you."

"I know. The grocer hates me. He barely looks at me let alone calls me by a name."

This time he leaned over her, dwarfing her, but she didn't flinch. "Why?" He couldn't understand how anyone could hate her.

"I was his daughter's gift for her eighth birthday. I lived in his house with him and Anna until..."

He waited for her to continue, staring at her tiny face and big eyes.

"Anna died. I didn't."

He used his thumb to wipe away the tears that slid down her cheeks. "What happened?"

"Carriage accident. No one's fault but Anna is gone." She wiped the rest of the tears away herself.

"He shouldn't blame you."

"He doesn't. I remind him of Anna. She was all he had. All I had." She flexed her claws. "I suppose I should be thankful. He could have taken me to the House Servants' Shelter or dumped me, but he isn't a cruel man."

"How long has it been since she died?"

"Ten years."

She'd been alone for ten years. He ran his thumb over her cheek. Her skin was soft under his rough touch. "What did

Anna call you?"

She shook her head. "I don't want you to call me that. That name is the past."

He leaned closer and brushed his lips against hers in a gentle taste. He'd never thought he'd end up with a House Servant. He'd never figured on ending up with anyone, but somehow they fit. "Sweet. That's what I'll call you." He kissed her again. "You taste sweet and you are the sweetest thing that I've ever met."

She smiled, her eyes glowing in the dark. "I like that name."

Her lips were open slightly, begging for his kiss. "How old are you?" If she were too young, he'd wait. He wasn't sure how he'd do it, but he would. He prayed that she wasn't too young.

"Seventeen."

He closed his eyes as he lowered his lips to hers. "Thank Araldo."

CHAPTER 9

BY THE NEXT MORNING Mutter's fever was back along with body aches. He'd been sick before but nothing like this. The pain was unbearable and it went on for days. The evenings were the only thing keeping him sane. Sweet would bathe him with cool water, her hands a haven from the agony. She'd feed him soup which he'd eat for her and then she'd curl up next to him and tell him stories from her days at the grocer's or from her past. Usually, she'd fall asleep and he'd stare into the darkness, focusing on her breathing to keep the pain at bay, but tonight the moon was full and he wasn't hurting as badly. His hand skimmed up and down her back. She snuggled closer. He loved her. He'd never thought he'd love anyone. He struggled with the words. He was strong. He could do this. He would do this. He'd be stronger than even he thought he could be, for her.

"I have to leave. It isn't safe for you if I stay."

She stiffened. Her silence was a stab to his heart, but he'd done the right thing. She pulled away and his arm clasped her tight, unable to let her leave.

"Let go." Her claws came out, digging into his wrist.

As far as pain went, it wasn't much, not compared to what he'd been going through. He should release her, but he couldn't. She clawed him on the side, catching a tender spot and he gasped. His hold loosened and she scurried away but he snatched her around the waist, pulling her to him, her back to his front.

"Don't be mad," he said. "I have to go. You know that."

"Then leave." There were tears in her voice.

"Come with me." His lips brushed against her ear. He hadn't meant to say the words, although they'd danced through his head every time he'd considered leaving. Now they were out in the open.

"Really?" She stopped struggling.

"I understand if you don't want to." It was asking a lot from her to abandon her home and travel with him.

Somehow, she spun in his arms and her lips were on his, kissing him. His hand dug into her hair, adjusting her to his needs.

"Is that a yes?" He murmured against her mouth.

"Yes. Definitely, yes." She playfully slapped his chest.

He leaned on an elbow. "It will be dangerous."

"No, it won't." Her fingers stopped his protest. "I've been thinking about it."

"Really?" He hadn't expected that. Now, he couldn't stop from smiling. "Since when?"

"It doesn't matter." She blushed slightly. He leaned down for a kiss but she pushed him away. "Pay attention. I've been hording some food, the stuff that doesn't rot."

"Won't you get caught?"

"No. The grocer allows me a certain amount. I've been eating some of the stuff I'm supposed to throw away." She gave him a quick kiss. "Now, stop distracting me."

"What did I do?" He acted offended but he was thrilled that he had distracted her enough for a kiss.

"We can leave in a few days, if you're feeling up to it."

"We can go tomorrow. I'll make it." He'd force himself. Every day that he stayed put her in danger. The Guards may not be hunting him but Ableson and Conguise would be.

"No. I need a little more time. We'll leave at dusk and head to the Lake of Sins." She sat up, almost trembling with eagerness. "We'll be safe there. Everyone avoids the place."

He'd heard stories of the Lake of Sins, every child had, but the place held a fascination for her. She and Anna had read everything that they'd found about the area, including the history of the town. It seemed like a pleasant place if you could ignore the superstitions. "It'll be perfect. We can swim and run through the woods, eating what we catch. I love the water." He kissed her.

Her fingers ran into his hair and then down his back. "I hate the water. You'll have to swim on your own, but I'll hunt with you and prepare what we kill. I want to learn how to cook."

"I'll build you a house with a kitchen. Anything you want." He winced as her fingers trailed over his ribs.

She examined his skin where her fingers had touched. "I cut you. I'm sorry."

There were four thin gashes on his chest. He didn't recall her cutting him or even touching him there. She leaned down and kissed the wounds. He didn't remember much after that.

Mutter's fever didn't return, but the headaches did. Even the slightest light made him almost scream in pain. He'd bury his head in the blankets and pray for the dark. He was always better at night. Once they left, they'd have to find a place to camp for the day. He would not be able to travel in the light. This sickness could not last much longer. He had to get better, for her.

He was dozing on the blankets, counting the time until evening when the bells over the door chimed and his eyes flew open. He sniffed. The professor was here. He staggered to his feet, still naked. He leaned against the wall as he moved across the room. She'd brought him clean clothes but he hadn't been well enough to use them. He braced himself against the sink as he pulled on his pants. He grabbed the shirt and stumbled to the door. He rested his head against the frame, listening. The professor was chatting with the grocer. Every word was clear. Conguise was looking for his lost Guard.

Mutter wanted to let Sweet know why he was leaving, but there was no time. He'd return tonight, when it was safe. He left the room and crept out the back door, the sunlight hitting him in the face and sending pain slicing through his head. He dropped to his knees, chest heaving as if he'd run for miles.

"The professor said you'd be here." Laddie, one of Conguise's Guards, grasped Mutter under the arm.

He looked up into Laddie's sad, brown eyes. "Please, let me go."

"We can't." Laddie pulled him to his feet as two other Guards surrounded him.

Instinct surged through him. Trapped. Danger. Flee. Fight. Sentences no longer formed in his mind, just words and red hot, burning pain. He lashed out, his fist connecting with Laddie's jaw and sending the older Guard stumbling backward. He spun around, hitting the other Guards. They all went down and he ran. He was almost to the alley when something jabbed him in the back. He kept moving. He'd get to the forest, the water. Lose his scent. Come back for Sweet later. He stumbled, his legs rubbery. He collapsed, his face hitting the ground. Footsteps approached and stopped by his head.

"Professor, he's still awake," said Ableson. "I don't understand. I gave him the same dose that we used on the others."

Another set of footsteps. Male hands ran over his chest, searching, studying. They lingered on his side, the scratches. He gasped as pain passed through the numbness.

"He's been without the stabilizer for over two weeks. The transformation has progressed faster than in any of the others," said Conguise. "Give him another shot. We can't have him waking up on the way back."

CHAPTER 10

WHEN MUTTER CAME TO he was back in his cage and Ableson sat at the table, looking into a microscope. It was almost as if he'd never left, except now he missed Sweet. He'd never see her again.

The door opened and the professor entered. "Has he regained consciousness?"

The two Almightys peered into the cage. He sat up. No reason to pretend. No reason for anything anymore.

"How are you feeling?" asked the professor, pen in hand.

"Better." They didn't seem angry which was surprising.

The professor raised his brow.

"My headache is gone."

"Body?"

"Still hurts." They acted concerned, but if they cared about him, they'd let him leave.

"Hmm." The professor turned and looked into the microscope. "These are his latest samples?"

"Yes," said Ableson.

Conguise prepared a syringe and approached the cage. "Give me your arm."

He was done taking orders. It no longer mattered if he was sent back to the shelter. All he wanted was freedom and Sweet. They weren't going to let him have either.

"Do you want the pain to come back?" asked the professor.

He couldn't take that, not without Sweet here with him. He put his arm through the cage and bit his lip as the fluid entered his body.

"Draw his blood every four hours," said the professor as he left.

Once the door closed, Ableson faced him. "You shouldn't have run."

"Sorry." He wasn't but that was what the Almighty wanted to hear.

"I thought we were friends. I trusted you." Ableson stepped over to his cage.

"I needed exercise, to run and swim. I lost track of time." He glanced down, trying to look repentant. "I was afraid to come back." If Ableson moved a little closer, he could wrap his hands around the Almighty's neck and squeeze until Ableson's eyes popped from his skull.

"Don't lie to me. I know about the Servant."

His head snapped upward. He should avert his gaze but he couldn't bring himself to do it. "What did you do to her?"

"Nothing."

"If anything happens to her—"

"What will you do locked in this cage?"

The words hit him like a punch to the gut. He breathed deeply trying to control his temper.

"You should have told me that you had the urge to mate. We were planning on bringing you female companionship if—"

"I don't want just any mate."

"Do you think it matters what you want?" Ableson looked at him, incredulous. "You betrayed...not just me but this entire project. Conguise will never give me a chance to bond with one of you again. According to him, it didn't work. It will be years before he listens to any of my ideas." He turned and walked back to his desk.

Mutter dropped on his pallet and prayed that Sweet was okay. He closed his eyes. In his mind she was fine. They were together at the Lake of Sins. Maybe, he could pretend to be dead like the Voice had said the others did. He slowed his breathing but his chest still rose and fell. It was no use.

The next morning when the professor arrived, he glanced at Mutter and then Ableson. Ableson shook his head. Conguise looked at the slide under the microscope and then the two stepped into the hallway, closing the door behind them.

"His metabolism is increasing too fast," said the professor.

"We should give him more stabilizer—"

"We have. It isn't working. This process can't be reversed. You've seen the X-rays and blood tests. There is nothing we can do but move forward." The professor's voice was tired.

"But he hadn't had that much serum before he ran." Ableson was almost pleading. "How can it happen this quickly?"

Mutter moved toward the bars, closer to the words. They were talking about him, they had to be. What couldn't they reverse? He felt stronger than ever. He wanted to get out of this cage and run and fight and find Sweet.

"He went too long without the stabilizer. We can mark this down to a lesson learned. The cocktail acts faster than we thought," said the professor. "And your bonding idea does not work."

"That's not true. It was working," said Ableson. "I underestimated the metamorphosis process."

"You blame this on the process?"

"Yes, if he were only a Guard, he would have stayed. We have a connection."

"Enough," said the professor. "I let you test your theory and it didn't work. There is no shame in that. Many of our theories prove to be false."

"But it will work. I swear. I just have to try again."

"No. Move him tonight and start the hunt for another subject," said the professor.

They came back inside and began their rounds around the room.

Mutter waited for his shot, but they skipped his cage so he went over to his blankets. They were taking him somewhere else, somewhere unknown and he didn't like it. However, it might give him a chance to escape and if the opportunity presented itself, he'd kill them before he left.

"You need to eat your dinner." Ableson glanced at the door. "Please. Before the professor arrives."

He glared at the Almighty. They didn't understand anything about the other classes. "I can smell the poison."

"What? No." Ableson's pale cheeks flushed.

He picked up the plate and held it out to the Almighty. "You take a bite first and then I'll eat."

Ableson shook his head. "The meat's too rare for me."

The door opened and the two burly Guards, Laddie and Jorge came into the room.

"Eat. Please, trust me," whispered Ableson.

He didn't, not at all. He dropped the plate on the floor.

Ableson sighed. "He refuses to eat."

Jorge nodded and left the room.

Mutter wasn't scared. He was strong, powerful. They should fear him. As soon as the cage door opened, he'd attack. He didn't care if he died; in death he'd have freedom.

The Guard returned with a gun. Mutter couldn't stop a slight quiver from racing through him. No one was supposed to have guns. The gun would eliminate his chance to attack, to take at least one of them with him.

The professor entered. He signaled to someone in the hallway and then closed the door behind him. "I see you aren't hungry."

Mutter remained silent.

"I was thinking about your bonding theory," said the professor.

Emotions flashed across Ableson's face. Surprise, hope and then confusion settled in to stay.

"You may be on to something, but I think you overestimated his bond with you." The professor began to pace. "Like you said, you didn't have enough time although some bonds take less time than others." Conguise glanced at Mutter. "Next time, we should start with a younger subject and I don't know that living in the lab is right."

"I agree." Hope had replaced the confusion on Ableson's face. "I think the subject should live with me."

The professor chuckled. "I wouldn't go that far, not yet. There is still a lot we don't know, but"—he turned and faced Mutter—"we are going to learn." He walked to the cage. "Eat."

They couldn't command him. They were weak; he was strong. They could kill him, but he didn't care.

"One way or another, you will obey me."

Mutter didn't blink.

"Bring her in," said the professor.

Laddie opened the door and Scar, the female Guard who assisted in the lab, entered dragging someone behind her.

Fear, true fear raced down Mutter's spine. "Let her go."

Sweet saw him and struggled in the Guard's grasp. "Mutter!"

"Let her go," he repeated, rage replacing his fear.

"Eat," said the professor.

He pulled his eyes from Sweet and glared at Conguise. "Then you'll let her go?"

The professor shook his head, smiling triumphant. "No." He held up his hand to stop Mutter's complaint. "But, I will keep her safe."

"That's not good enough." Sweet didn't deserve to be in a cage, safe but alone.

"You have no idea what I can do to her." The professor waved at Jorge. "Shoot him."

"No," shouted Sweet. "Mutter, eat. Do what they say, please."

The Guard aimed the gun. Mutter glanced at the food. Ableson had said it wasn't poisoned. He didn't trust the Almighty but he had no choice. The gun would kill him and he couldn't risk Sweet being left on her own. He bent to pick up the meat when something struck him on the side.

"No!" Sweet clawed Scar's arm, but the Guard kept her hold.

Mutter dropped to his knees. His vision blurred and then went black. When he woke he was in another cage in a different room. His mouth was dry and his head ached. He sat up.

"Mutter." Sweet was in the cage next to his. She put her arms through the bars, reaching for him.

He tried to stand but was still dizzy so he crawled over to her. Her fingers ran over his face.

"I'm sorry," he said. "I shouldn't have gone to you. I knew it was dangerous. I was dangerous."

She yanked on his hair. "This is not your fault. It's theirs." She glanced at the door, her hands trembling slightly. "What are they doing here?"

"I don't know."

"The things in the other cages..."

There was a soft overhead light but the room was mostly dark. Eyes glowed from the other enclosures, watching them. In a large cell in the corner several House Servants huddled, chains around their necks hooked to the front bars of the cage. Something ran across the enclosure directly across from him, tap, tap, tapping as it moved. He knew that sound. Goosebumps raised on his arms. He could smell his and Sweet's fear. The things in the other cages began to move restlessly. So could they. He stuck his arms through the bars, pulling her as close as he could, for once, thankful for the cage keeping them safe.

The next morning the door opened and the professor turned on the bright overhead lights. "Good, you're awake."

Conguise, Ableson, Laddie, Jorge and Scar entered the room.

Mutter pulled himself to his feet, pushing Sweet behind him as much as possible. "Let her go and I'll do anything you ask. I won't run away. I'll eat anything you want."

"Oh, Mutter. You really believe that don't you?" Conguise shook his head at Ableson. "Such naïve creatures."

"I swear to you. I will obey."

The professor walked to the cage that housed the House Servants. "Keeping your...companion is a much better way of ensuring your obedience." He motioned for the Guards to come to him.

"I will fight you every step of the way, unless you free her."

"Don't." Sweet grabbed his arm, her claws sinking in slightly.

"I think he needs to see what fate awaits his friend if he doesn't cooperate," said the professor.

"Aranea18 needs to be fed," said Ableson.

The professor's eyes darted toward Mutter and Sweet. "Excellent. She is one of my favorites."

The Servants in the cage trembled and shifted as far back in their enclosure as they could. Some even tried to pull their heads through their collars. Laddie unlocked one of the chains and dragged the Servant to the front of the cage.

"No, please, please, no," begged the elderly, female Servant.

Scar opened the door and Laddie pulled the Servant out of the enclosure.

"Don't do this, please." The Servant fell to the floor, sobbing and begging.

No one paid any attention to her pleas as Laddie dragged her across the room. Jorge and Scar followed. They stopped at the cell directly across from Mutter. Jorge pointed a gun at whatever was in the cage. Scar moved to the door, key in hand. The Guards waited, ears tipped toward the professor.

"Now," said Conguise.

Scar opened the door as Laddie shoved the Servant inside the enclosure and slammed the cage door shut. The two Guards scurried across the room.

"No," screamed the Servant, eyes wide with fear as she tried to squeeze through the bars. "Please, let me out."

The sound of tapping was the first warning. Mutter's breath froze in his chest. The sound changed to almost a clatter and something appeared. It was the thing that had been caged next to him. The thing with the hairy arm except it wasn't an arm anymore. The creature had four long, thin, segmented legs, each with two claws on the end. It was fast, faster than anything he'd ever seen and it was on the Servant in a flash, wrapping two of its legs around her in an obscene embrace. As soon as it touched her, she quieted, but her mouth remained open in a silent scream.

Aranea18 turned and Mutter staggered backward, knocking into Sweet. The creature had eight eyes, two rows of four, and two large almost claw-like fangs protruding from near its mouth. The fangs opened wide, liquid dripping from the tips, and plunged into the Servant's chest, ribs cracking. A garbled scream penetrated the air and quickly died. Then the creature began to feed, sucking the fluids from the body which writhed in its grasp.

Sweets' claws sunk into his arm, had been there for some time, but he hadn't noticed. His heart slammed against his chest. The professor was right. He would do anything to keep her from that fate.

CHAPTER 11

THE NEXT FEW WEEKS passed as a blur for Mutter. The Almightys had stopped giving him the injections and his pain returned worse than before. Sometimes, he'd spend days vomiting, unable to eat or drink anything. Other times, the pain would be focused on a single part of his body. Always, Sweet would hold his head through the bars of the cage, whispering to him.

During the day when the Almightys were present, the stories she told were of her childhood or her time at the grocer's, but at night they would be of their escape. Often, there was a bit about their vengeance on Ableson and Conguise and how they would free the Servants who were food for the things in the cages, but there was always a part about their peaceful life at the Lake of Sins. Just them. Together with no Almightys.

Usually, her voice was enough to let him rest, but today the pain in his feet was mind splitting. He was drenched in sweat and his body trembled as blood trickled from the pores on his feet. It was late and Sweet had passed out, exhausted. He eased from her arms and curled in a ball, trying to keep his moans quiet so as not to disturb her. The blood dripped faster as the bones in his feet snapped and stretched, his skin tearing to accommodate the transformation. He stuck his arm in his mouth and bit down to keep from crying out.

Early the next morning when Ableson arrived, he took one look at Mutter and ran out of the room. A few moments later he returned with the professor, Laddie and Jorge.

"It's time," said the professor.

"Mutter," whispered Sweet, her arms reaching for him through the bars.

He crawled to her.

"Come here," said the professor.

"I love you." He held Sweet's eyes for a moment.

She clasped onto his arm but he stood breaking her hold. They both knew what would happen if he didn't obey. He staggered to the front of the cage, shaking from the pain in his feet.

Jorge held a gun on him as Laddie pointed one at Sweet.

The professor put the key in the lock but didn't turn it. "Aranea18 is due for a feeding."

He nodded his understanding and Conguise opened the cage door.

"Come." The professor walked out of the room.

"Mutter," her voice was a soft whisper.

He sent one last desperate look at her and then followed the Almighty. The two Guards and Ableson followed him. They went down a hallway and then entered another room. It was large with a table and chair in the center. On the table was a monitor, notepads, pens and a microscope. Toward the back of the room was a large tank filled with water.

He couldn't pull his gaze away from that crystal clear water. He wanted, no needed to sink into it. It would make him better; it would take away his pain.

"Get in," said the professor.

He glanced suspiciously at the Almightys.

"It's okay," said Ableson. "The water is for you."

For once he was glad to obey as he stumbled to the tank, almost falling as he tried to climb the stairs. At the top, he slipped into the water. It was cool, easing the burning in his feet and body. Blood still ran from between his toes, causing the water to turn cloudy. That was better anyway. Clear water was dangerous. Anyone could see him.

The professor unlocked a panel on the wall and pushed a few buttons. A cage dropped from the ceiling surrounding the tank of water and creating a large enclosure inside the room. "Get the female."

The two Guards left.

"Should I divide my time between here and the other lab?" asked Ableson.

"No. Stay here. I'll get Tantiori and Truent to assist with the other projects."

"Do you think that's wise? I mean with Truent's upbringing and everything."

The professor frowned. "You're right. I'll get Parson instead. He's young, but bright. I'll be back to relieve you in a few hours." The professor turned and left the room.

Ableson sat on the chair, and took his notepad from his pocket. "Don't worry Mutter, your pain will be gone soon. Then all you'll feel is strong and powerful. I promise."

He stared at the Almighty through the water. He had let himself sink to the bottom. It was nice below the surface. He could still hear Ableson but the sound wasn't as sharp and offensive. He waited as long as he could, surfaced for another breath and then sank again. The next time, when his lungs screamed for oxygen, there was a sharp pain in his chest and a great whoosh of air filled his lungs. Blood oozed from the slashes in his sides. He inhaled and gasped, swimming to the surface.

Ableson chuckled. "You'll need to learn to breathe through your gills when under water." His smile faded a bit. "Don't feel bad. They all make that mistake."

He trembled as another pain ricocheted through his neck. His fingers found four slashes on each side of his chest and two on each side of his neck. He dove under the water, into safety where the pain was dulled.

A few minutes later when the Guards returned with Sweet, he swam to the surface.

"Where should we put her?" asked Jorge.

"In the cage." Ableson jotted notes on a pad of paper.

"With him? He'll—"

"We don't know what he'll do." Ableson's voice was harsh. "But we'll learn."

Laddie opened the door.

"Mutter!" cried Sweet, as she ran into the cage.

He climbed out of the tank and raced toward her, stumbling a bit. His legs were unsteady under him. He stopped, taking her hands in his. She stared downward, her eyes wide and face pale. He followed her gaze. His feet were different.

The toes had elongated and widened. Webbed skin grew between them.

"What have they done to you?" her voice trembled.

He opened his mouth gasping for breath. Spots appeared before him, marring Sweet's lovely face. He needed oxygen. He staggered backward; she grabbed him under his arm, steadying him. The slits on the side of his throat opened and oxygen filled his lungs and cleared the passage to his nose. She stared at his throat and then raised her hand to touch the slashes on his chest. He was changing just like the Voice had told him. He was becoming a monster. Dangerous. He shoved her away and stumbled toward the tank. His webbed feet tangled in his haste and he fell.

"Mutter!" She rushed to his side.

"Leave me." He crawled away from her.

She didn't follow as he made his way up the stairs and disappeared into the water. He remained submerged for days, weeks perhaps. She sat near the tank, staring at him through the glass. He was glad when the pain arrived because with it came the blood, making it harder for her to see him. He didn't want her to look at him. He was a monster. He glared at the professor who sat at the table, taking notes and staring at the monitor. They had done this to him. He glanced at Sweet who leaned against the tank, arms wrapped around her knees, drifting in and out of sleep. They had taken more from him than he'd ever thought he could have. For this, they would pay. One day, they would pay.

Scar entered carrying a tray of food. She slid it into the cage. Sweet walked over and picked it up. Three times a day, she brought the food to him, placing the tray on the side of the tank. She'd eat her dinner, talking to him like before and trying to coax him to eat. Eventually, she'd curl up and fall asleep. Then, he'd swim to the surface and eat the meat.

"Leave it," ordered the professor.

"But, he needs food."

"Then he'll have to come and get it."

She glanced back at the tank and took a small portion for herself, leaving the tray where it sat.

His stomach rumbled but he would not leave the water. The pain was less and less now, but that was because he was different. His body had changed. His hair was gone. His spine had stretched, giving him a powerful tail and his fingers were now like his feet, webbed and larger. All of these changes made swimming easier, but outside the water he'd be clumsy and vulnerable. He couldn't bear seeing the disgust in her eyes when she saw him clearly for the first time. He fought his hunger and waited.

Late that night, when Ableson dozed and Sweet slept, he climbed out of the tank, the scent of the somewhat rotting meat dragging him from the safety of the water. The trays of food from breakfast, lunch and dinner sat near the cage door. He crept over to them and tried to pick up the meat but his flipper-hands didn't work like his old hands. His hunger was almost overwhelming. He glanced at Sweet. She hadn't moved. He sunk to his knees and lowered his face to the tray, swallowing the food as quickly as he could get it into his mouth. A slight hiccup caused him to spin around. Sweet stared at him through the darkness. He jumped to his feet, hitting the trays with his tail and causing a loud crash. He refused to look at her as he tromped back to the stairs, his stride wide and large to accommodate his flipper-feet.

"Oh my, the professor will want to know about your progress." Ableson raced from the room.

Mutter was almost to the tank when Sweet caught up to him.

"Stop, please."

He moved faster, but she was quicker than him now and the touch of her fingers on his arm made him hesitate. Her hand trembled. His skin was different too, gray and cold and scaly.

She moved in front of him, never removing her hand. It was what kept his feet in place.

"Oh Mutter, what have they done to you?"

There was only sadness in her voice not disgust, but he wasn't brave enough to raise his eyes to hers.

She ran her hands over his body, lingering at the slashes on his chest and neck. "Does it hurt?"

He shook his head.

"Good." Her fingers drifted to his chin, applying pressure to raise his head.

He refused to budge.

She put both hands on his shoulders, stood on tiptoe and kissed his chin. His head jerked back at the contact.

"I love you." Her pale green eyes searched his.

"I...mon...ster." His voice was raspy and the words didn't sound like they had before.

"No. You're my Mutter." Her hand rested on his cheek.

The door opened and the two Almightys entered the room. He stepped away from her but she blocked his path.

"Ignore them. They are not important."

He'd always been stronger than her, and now his body was entire muscle. Yet, her gentle touch controlled him. He wanted to flee so no one could see him, but she owned his heart so he stayed. She ran her hand up his chest and around his neck, pulling him down toward her. He moved so that he blocked her from the Almightys' view.

She kissed him, her lips sweet and warm. His webbed hands trembled at his sides, yearning to touch her, but he wouldn't. She shifted back, adding a little space between their lips.

"Why?" He asked, searching her face for the truth.

"I didn't care what you looked like before, why do you think I would now?"

"Be...fore, I ug...ly, now I mon...ster."

She shook her head, tears pooling in her eyes. "No. You were never ugly to me and you are *not* a monster." She shifted to look past him at the Almightys. "They are the monsters." Her voice was quiet so only he could hear, but her eyes were filled with hatred.

"No. They hurt you." He moved to block her from them.

"I don't care what they do to me." She rested her head against his heart. "Not anymore."

He couldn't wait any longer. He touched her back, softly at first, but when she only burrowed closer to him, he pulled her tight. "I care."

They stood like that for a while and then they sat down near the tank, hidden as much as possible from the Almightys' view. He'd never understand how she could still care for him, but he'd take it without question. The Almightys muttered to each other about how this was possible and how long it would last before he'd kill her. They thought that they were being quiet but both he and Sweet heard every word.

"I ne...ver hurt you. Ev...er," he whispered.

"I know." She snuggled closer.

The days passed. The Almightys still refused to let Sweet bring him the food. He no longer cared if anyone saw him, but to annoy them he'd wait until night, after Ableson had fallen asleep, to creep out and eat. The Almightys soon tired of this and began taking the tray from the previous meal when they brought the next one.

He'd just finished his dinner and was lying next to Sweet by the tank.

"You should start eating at least one other meal." She ran her hand across his ribs. "You're losing weight."

"No hun...gry."

She patted his stomach and it rumbled. "Liar."

He smiled at her and she leaned up and kissed him. "I love your smile. I can still see the old Mutter there."

He blinked a couple of times to keep the tears at bay. His jaw had started hurting, a lot. His face would change next.

"Are you feeling okay? Do you need to get back into the tank?" She sat up.

He nodded. It was the simplest explanation and it was partially true. Every night, he spent less and less time out of the water, which meant less and less time with her. She stayed by the tank when he was inside of it, but that wasn't the same as holding her.

"Your skin's dry. You should go." She smiled sadly. "They need to clean the tank; I can barely see you in there anymore."

He ran his hand over her face, memorizing the look in her eyes. He may never see it again. Tonight, his face, the only part of Mutter left, would disappear. He wrapped her in his arms and kissed her for a long time. When he pulled back, she was looking at him curiously.

"Are you sure you're okay?" Her eyes searched his for the truth.

Tomorrow, she'd answer that question for him. He stood and slipped into the water, sinking to the bottom. She stared at the tank for a long time before falling asleep.

The cool water soothed and invigorated him. He swam to burn up his energy and to keep from thinking about the coming transformation and what she would think of his new face. Would she still kiss him, love him or would she finally see the monster he had become? Pain lanced through his jaw and blood drifted into the water. He stared at her for one long moment and then turned away, holding his head in his hands as his tears mingled with the blood and water.

CHAPTER 12

THE NEXT DAY MUTTER refused to get out of the tank. The blood from this last change had dirtied the water so much he was positive that as long as he stayed away from the sides she couldn't see him, and there was no way he was going to let her see him. He'd starve first. His face was a mess, all mouth and rows of sharp teeth. He truly was a monster now.

On the third day, Ableson succumbed to Sweet's pleas and allowed her to drop food into the tank. Mutter's resolve to starve faded as the meat drifted past him. He snapped his jaw, snatching a hunk of meat and chewed, but his teeth were different. They couldn't grind the food. He tipped his head back and swallowed. It was dry and tasteless. He let the rest sink to the bottom.

He wasn't sure how many days passed. Ableson and Conguise constantly scribbled in their notepads and talked in whispers outside the room. He refused to listen. Nothing they said mattered anymore. Sweet continued to attempt to coax him out of the tank. She would eventually drop the meat into the water and then sit by the side, crying. He hated being the cause of her tears, but if he let her see him it would be worse.

A ripple in the water drew his gaze upward. Something dangled above. He drifted toward it, saliva pooling in his mouth. This was food, alive and filled with blood. His body almost vibrated with the urge to attack, but he had to move carefully or it would escape. He studied it from below. It was small and skinny, legs splashing in the water as it clung to a rope over the center or his tank. He moved closer. The splashing increased. His muscles tensed and he flew upward breaching the water and wrapping his arms around the creature. A scream pierced the air as he pulled his dinner from the rope and into the water.

"Mutter, no. Let him go!" Sweet pounded on the glass. "He's just an old Servant. Let him go."

He looked at the creature in his grasp. It was a House Servant, but he hated Servants, except Sweet. His eyes darted to her. She continued to scream, slamming her fists against the tank. He released his hold and his prey swam to the surface. Sweet grabbed the old Servant's hands and dragged him out of the water.

The Servant ran across the enclosure and grasped the bars of the cage. "Please, let me out of here!"

The professor nodded and Laddie opened the door, letting the Servant out, before quickly shutting it again. Mutter's stomach rumbled and he swam to the bottom and ate the rotting meat. It wasn't too bad.

After that, he dozed in the water. He'd found a small shelf where he could stick the tips of his flipper-feet to keep him from floating to the surface.

"Mutter," called Sweet in a whisper. "Ableson's sleeping. Come to me. I miss you."

She was looking over the edge of the tank. He could grab her in an instant and pull her under, but she hated getting wet.

"I saw you today and I don't care about your face. Please, come out of the water."

He didn't believe her. It had all happened so fast that she couldn't have gotten a good look at him.

"You *will* pay for this." She jumped into the water.

She was inside his tank. Here he was power. He swam past her, letting his large body brush against her feet so she'd understand how helpless she was in his domain. Then, she'd leave. Instead, she ducked under the water her hands brushing across his leg.

She resurfaced, gasping for breath. "Mutter, stop playing and hold me."

Hold her. Hold her. The words echoed through him and he drifted up until only his eyes and top of his head were above the surface.

"Please. I can't swim well." She held out her arms.

He would let her see his face and give her the chance to flee although he wasn't sure that he could let her go. He emerged, head and shoulders, from the water. She gasped and horror filled her eyes, sending a lance to his heart. He started to sink, to hide when she splashed over to him, wrapping her arms around his neck.

"How many times do I have to tell you that I love you? You!" She slapped the side of his head. "I don't care what you look like." She clasped his shoulders, trying to shake him, but he didn't budge. "Don't make me tell you again."

He nodded. Words were hard now.

"Are you going to hold me, or are you going to let me drown you stubborn fool?"

He rolled his eyes at her dramatics as he wrapped his arms around her, pulling her close. Her heart beat was soft and fluttery, his large and pounding, but hers held all the power. He rested his face against her neck. He wasn't sure how long they stayed like this, but soon, she began to tremble. The water was too cold for her. He used his tail to move them to the side.

"No. I won't leave you." She wrapped her arms tighter around him.

He tapped his chest and motioned toward the top.

"You're getting out too?"

He nodded.

"And you're okay out of the water? I don't want you to get sick."

He started to smile but stopped. She hadn't seen all his teeth and he had a lot.

She leaned forward, her fingers lightly brushing over his lips. "I don't care."

She kissed him quick and then again, deeper. He pulled her close, kissing her back.

"Mine," he rasped.

"Mine," she whispered against his lips.

Mutter and Sweet fell into a pattern over the next few weeks. She would toss him the meat and he'd let it rot a bit before eating it. It wasn't what he wanted but it curbed his hunger and made her happy. What he wanted was the House Servant who the Almightys stuck on a rope and hung over the top of his tank. For her, he refused to take one but he couldn't help looking. He'd float just underneath them, waiting. Sweet would tell them that it was safe, that he wouldn't hurt them, but they never believed her. He didn't blame them. He was never sure whether he would grab them like he needed or let them go like she wanted. Eventually, they'd drop from exhaustion. Her voice would rise slightly as she'd tell them to swim to the side, and remind him that he did not want to hurt them. She was right. He didn't want to hurt them; he wanted to eat them.

After each escape, he'd swim in circles, his stomach aching and his mind grumbling. The food had been right there. Why had he let it go? Later, she'd call and he'd leave the tank and rest in her arms. That was when he remembered why he listened to her. She was his everything. Nothing else mattered. Not his desires, his hunger or his life. Only her.

Today, he floated in the tank, waiting for the Servant, his food, his offering. Maybe this time, the Servant would drown and he'd be able to satisfy his hunger.

When the professor entered the room, Ableson took one more glance at his notes and stood. "I need to speak with you."

"Then speak."

"Not here." Ableson shot a glance at the tank.

"He is well past understanding a word we say."

"I think you're wrong about that." Ableson held the door open for the professor and they both left.

Mutter glanced at Sweet who sat with her ears tipped toward the door as she sharpened her claws. He moved toward the front of the tank.

"He listens to her, so he has to understand us," said

Ableson. "She is the reason that he's not eating the...what we offer him."

"You could be right. I've never seen one wait this long to feed. The little meat that we give him can't be enough."

"It isn't. He's getting thinner. Too thin."

Sweet glanced toward the tank, concern in her pale eyes.

"Stop feeding him," said the professor.

"What? He'll starve."

"Or eat what we give him. Or kill her," said the professor.

"We don't want that. We are learning so much from these two, more than the others combined."

"Yes, but we need to push it. We need to know if hunger will break the bond. You don't want to have one under your command and find out too late that a few hunger pangs will cause it to turn on you. We need to know how far these bonds will stretch before breaking."

"I agree, but not like this."

"What do you propose?" The professor's voice was clipped. He did not like having his ideas questioned.

"We should bond with her and then add her to the project." Ableson lowered his voice. "If she is loyal to us, and he is loyal to her..."

Mutter swam to the top of the tank and pulled himself half out. Sweet was looking up at him, her face pale.

"If they turn me, I could be with you. Truly with you."

He shook his head. He wanted nothing more than to be with her again, but not like this. She was too good to be turned into a monster.

"We could escape and live at the Lake of Sins." She smiled. "In the Lake of Sins."

The Almightys' voices rose slightly, drawing their attention back to the door.

"I'm sure that turning her is the answer," said Ableson.

"No. Not yet anyway."

"Why? We can't wait much longer or he'll starve, unless we increase his food."

"No. No more food. He will eat what we send him, her or nothing," said the professor.

"I think you're making a mistake."

"Perhaps, but it is *my* project." The professor's voice softened. "You picked well when you found him. We are learning a lot and I don't want to lose him, but you have to remember that these creatures are exceptional hunters with voracious appetites. He won't be able to withstand the temptation much longer. You'll see."

CHAPTER 13

IT HAD BEEN DAYS since the Almightys had allowed Mutter any food except what was dangled over his cage. At first, Sweet had begged Ableson, but when that didn't work she'd attempted to share her food. Conguise had caught her and had threatened to use her for food if she tried again.

The Almightys were right, hunger and the desire to kill waged war with his need to keep her happy. He stopped watching the offerings, hanging right out of his reach. It was too tempting. Instead, he'd circle the bottom looking for scraps of meat, but after the second day there was nothing.

The latest Servant immediately dropped into the water and splashed to the side. Word must have gotten out that this monster refused to kill. Mutter's muscles tensed and he hit his head against the side of the tank over and over to keep from grabbing that leg and pulling the struggling creature into his webbed embrace. As soon as the feet left the tank, he sunk to the bottom, his stomach clenching.

That night, like every night, she called to him, her voice a siren's song that he could not refuse. His arms trembled as he attempted to pull himself out of the tank.

"Mutter!" She grabbed him around the chest, struggling to drag him out of the water.

He didn't want to die at the bottom of the tank alone, like he'd been most of his life. He surged upward and out, collapsing on the floor. He would die in her arms.

She snuggled close to him, pulling his head to her chest. "Oh Mutter, I'm so sorry."

He wanted to ask what she was sorry for, but couldn't form the words. He shook his head instead.

"I said that I loved you no matter what but I didn't understand."

He stiffened. Did she no longer love him?

She took his head in her hands and raised his face to hers. "I love you. I loved Mutter the Guard and now I love Mutter the"—she smiled, tears in her eyes—"I don't know what you are, but I love you."

He rested his forehead against hers.

"Tomorrow, when they...you need to eat." Her fingers trembled against his jaw.

He raised his head, staring into her eyes.

"It's okay." She kissed him.

He pulled her close. Tears ran down her cheeks long after her breathing became steady from slumber.

The next day, he was still weak but anticipation coursed through him. When Ableson awoke, Sweet was waiting at the cage door for him.

"You need to bring him a...he'll eat," she said.

"How do you know?"

"I told him that it was okay." Her voice cracked.

"Thank you." Ableson stood. "Really. I"—he looked at the tank—"he's a favorite of mine."

"I have one condition."

Mutter stopped swimming. What was she doing?

"A condition?" There was humor in the Almighty's voice.

"Yes." She glanced back at the tank, an apology in her eyes. "I want you to change me. I want to be with him."

He flew out of the water, all exhaustion replaced by fear for her. He raced toward them, his arms swinging.

"I don't think he agrees." Ableson backed away from the cage.

She glared at the Almighty. "I want a shot or I'll tell him not to eat. I'll let him die and I'll die too." She turned to face Mutter. "Do you hear me? I'll stop eating too."

He shook his head and then put his hands on her shoulders and shook her. He opened his mouth to force a word out, but she placed her fingers on his lips. It was their secret that he could still speak.

"I want to be with you. We can't live like this."

He shook his head again. He didn't want this for her.

"They will never let me go. They will feed me to one of those things once you die."

Mutter glared at Ableson and rushed the cage. The Almighty tripped in his haste to get away, falling on the ground.

She turned toward Ableson. "Tell him. Tell him the truth. If he dies, what will you do with me?"

Ableson stood and brushed off his pants. "She's right. You are the only thing keeping her alive. The professor will kill her if you die."

"Bring him something to eat, but first bring me the serum."

"This has to be our secret."

She nodded and Ableson turned and left the room.

She took Mutter's hand and led him to the tank. "You need to eat and get strong. Once I change we'll escape. I know this area. The sewer beneath us leads to tunnels and the tunnels lead to freedom."

He pointed at the enclosure.

"Don't worry about the cage. All I need is a bone and some time. I can pick that lock."

He pointed to her and then himself, shaking his head.

"It was bad enough when we were Servant and Guard but I will not flee with you and live this half-life. Not when we can be the same."

He touched his face, hands, and chest. "Hurt."

"I don't care about the pain. It'll pass." She kissed him. "Now, get back into the tank."

Ableson entered the room and jogged over to the enclosure. "Hurry, the professor is on his way."

She stuck her arm through the bars and the Almighty injected her with the serum. The door opened. Sweet stepped back as Ableson slipped the syringe into his pocket.

"She says that she's convinced him to eat." Ableson turned toward the professor. "I've ordered Jorge to bring a Servant right away."

The professor strolled closer to the cage, eyes never leaving Sweet. "And you believe that he will listen to you?"

"Yes," she said.

Jorge entered the room, dragging an elderly, male House Servant. The Servant didn't put up much of a fight. None of them did anymore. Not since it had become common knowledge that this monster didn't kill.

"We'll soon see," said the professor.

Jorge and the Servant climbed the portable stairs that stood next to the enclosure. Jorge turned on the machine that lowered a small cage from the ceiling. Mutter circled near the surface, his stomach raging. As soon as the Servant saw the shadow in the water he froze.

"Please, don't do this." The Servant began to struggle.

"This is gonna happen." Jorge shoved him into the cage. "I suggest you hold on."

The Guard pressed another button and the cage slid along the chains. As soon as it was over the center of the tank, Jorge flipped a switch and the bottom dropped out of the enclosure. The Servant clung to the rope that hung from the ceiling as the cage was lifted into the rafters.

Sweet leaned on her elbows over the top of the tank, looking down at her clenched fists. "It's o...okay. You c...can drop. He won't..." Her claws dug into her palms and tiny droplets of blood fell into the tank.

Mutter smelled the blood in the air, but he could almost taste it once it was in the water. He swam faster. He couldn't wait for this Servant to drop. He glanced at Sweet. She nodded, tears streaming down her cheeks. He dove to the bottom and then upward as fast as he could. He was weak and tired, but excitement of the kill surged through him as he shot from the water. The Servant screamed as Mutter grabbed him around the thighs, yanking him from the safety of the rope and pulling him into the murky depths. He spun and spun until the Servant hung loose in his arms. He sank his teeth into the creature's gut. Blood poured into the water as he tore off chunks and feasted.

When he was full, he pulled the rest of the carcass to the bottom and stuffed it under a small ledge. He'd eat again later. Now, he wanted Sweet. He wanted to hold her close. He swam to the surface, the water dark and full of blood. Fear tripped across his spine. She'd seen everything. It was one thing to say it was okay and another to see it in all its glory and still feel the same. He hesitated, far enough below that she probably couldn't see him. She stood at the edge of the tank, staring into the water. Her very presence drew him closer. There must have been some movement in the water, for she opened her arms. It was all the invitation he needed. He raced to the surface and climbed out of the tank and into her embrace.

"He fed," said Ableson, fear and shock in his voice.

"So, he did," said the professor. "He's strong too. I wouldn't have thought that he would've been able to make that jump, not after so many days without food."

"I told you, he's a fighter," said Ableson.

The professor walked closer to the cage and looked directly at Mutter. "You've surprised me and that doesn't happen very often. I didn't believe that you could understand us at this point in your transformation."

Even though they were far away from the Almightys, Mutter couldn't stop himself from shifting so that Sweet was behind him.

"I don't understand this bond between the two of you. If you were, had been, both Guards I could see, but interclass mating is pointless. You can't reproduce."

His body trembled. He wanted to tear the professor's head

off his shoulders. She ran her hand up his back, soothing him.

"Ableson wants me to change her. He thinks you might be able to produce offspring."

She stepped out from behind Mutter. "I want that too."

"Do you?" The professor studied her curiously.

"Yes."

"Why?"

"What are my options? You won't set me free." She moved closer to the Almighty, Mutter right behind her. "So, I either change or become food. I prefer to change."

"You're intelligent. Reasonable. We could use that quality in our...projects."

"Then let's start the process," said Ableson.

"Hmm. His commitment to her could hamper our progress."

"How?" asked Ableson. "Once changed, they will definitely mate. That alone is progress."

"If we change her and they can't reproduce it will set us back." His eyes pierced Mutter. "I'm starting to believe that he won't move on to another if she is available. Still...." The professor began to pace. "She is willing and intelligent." He stopped pacing, his eyes falling on Sweet this time. "I could show you the options that you have. You don't have to become"—he waved his hand at Mutter—"him."

"I don't want to be something else. I want to be with him." She wrapped her arm around Mutter, blushing slightly. "I promise. We will mate."

The professor moved closer to the cage. "But you are a Servant and he was a Guard. In your original state you could not produce viable offspring. Even once you've changed, you retain some qualities of your former self. We have a better chance with breeding between two Guards or two Servants who have transformed. Do you understand?"

"I do." Her voice cracked. "But please, let us try."

"I'll think about it." Conguise walked to the table and sat down.

"Professor, we can separate them if it doesn't work," said Ableson.

"I said I'd think about it." The professor opened his notebook. "Tell the Guards to clean the tank."

"The Guards are cleaning Aranea18's cage." Ableson's face paled.

"Ah, yes. They have repairs to make too. That will take some time." He tapped his finger on the monitor. "As soon as they are done then. I can't see anything in that water now, even on the camera."

Mutter looked at Sweet. She shrugged. He should have suspected that they had cameras in his tank. He could find them and break them, but it no longer mattered if they saw him. All that mattered was her. He took her hand and led her to the side of the tank that was the farthest away from the Almightys. He sat down, pulling her close. He touched the dried tears on her cheeks. "So..ar..ee."

She kissed him as her hand rubbed his stomach. "Don't be. You ate. We all have to eat." She glanced at the tank. "Something always dies." She kissed him again and rested her head against his heart.

The next morning as soon as the professor left, Ableson waved her over. She gave him her arm and he took some of her blood. He walked to the table to view it under the microscope.

"How...how's it going?" she asked.

"Slow." He looked up from the microscope. "I mean, normal, which is good, but...if the professor finds out that I'm doing this he's not going to be happy."

"He can't stop the process, can he?"

"Up to a point it is reversible then it is manageable and then"—he stared at the tank—"well, there is nothing we can do but let it progress until the end."

"Then hurry it along to that phase."

Mutter didn't want them to hurry this process. It might not work right. The pain he'd gone through had been almost unbearable. He couldn't imagine it happening faster, with no break. He rose, head and torso, out of the water and barked, a hoarse dry sound.

"Holy...I never saw one do that before," exclaimed Ableson.

She ignored the Almighty and faced Mutter. "It's the only way." She turned back to Ableson. "The professor won't kill me once I've changed will he?"

"No. I don't think so. He'll be angry and I'll be cleaning cages for months but he'll be too curious to see if you can produce young to kill you. The others refused to mate." He flushed. "I don't think we'll have that problem with the two of you."

"No, you won't."

"I'll give you another shot tonight, stronger."

That night as soon as Ableson fell asleep, Mutter retrieved a small bone from his tank and gave it to Sweet. She filed down the tip on the side of the stairs until it was thin and sharp. She tucked it into a small crevice under the tank when she was done.

"Now, all we have to do is wait for me to change."

He pulled her close, wishing he could go through this for her.

By the next morning, Sweet was running a high fever.

"This is normal, right?" She stood at the cage door while Ableson checked her vitals. "Mutter ran a fever for days when we were at the grocer's."

"Yes, this is part of the transformation." He glanced at the door. "Conguise will be here shortly. Try and stay hidden. You don't want to call attention to yourself if you can help it."

"Can it still be reversed?"

"I think so."

The Guards came in with the professor. Scar carried the gun. Sweet hurried to the back of the cage.

"Move the Servant to the other lab while you clean the tank," said the professor.

"I...I don't think we should do this today," said Ableson.

"Why not? The Guards finished Aranea18's enclosure last night."

"He's still weak. We should feed him at least once more before we tranquilize him."

"We need to observe him and we can't see anything in that water," said the professor.

"Ah...he spent most of the night at the top of the tank. Maybe, the water is too dirty even for him. We could use this time to see how they move at the surface." Ableson threw a desperate glance at Mutter.

He glared at the Almighty. If it weren't for Sweet, he'd go directly to the bottom, but instead, he'd be spending his day doing tricks at the top to enthrall the Almightys. He swam in a couple of circles and then used his tail to lift his torso out of the water and swam backward.

"Amazing," said the professor as he grabbed his notepad and began scribbling.

"Do you want us to clean the tank?" asked Laddie.

"Not today." The professor continued to write.

Ableson sent Mutter and Sweet a slight nod and then left.

Ableson glanced around as he entered the room. "Good evening, Professor. How's Mutter?" His voice was slightly shrill with nerves but the professor didn't notice.

"Very, very active." The professor smiled. "You should have an interesting night. If I didn't have plans with my daughter, I'd stay. The way he moves is fascinating. It's almost like he was born to water."

"Excellent." Ableson's lips trembled as he smiled, his eyes darting around the cage.

"I'll see you in the morning," said the professor as he left.

As soon as he was gone, Mutter crawled out of the tank and over to Sweet. She was curled in a ball, drenched in sweat and trembling from the fever. He picked her up, cradling her in his arms and carried her to the gate. He placed her on the ground and took a step back.

"You...you need to get back into the water," said Ableson.

He stared at the Almighty for several moments and then took another few steps back and waited.

"I'm not entering the cage until you're in the water."

He ran his flipper over Sweet's hair and then went to the tank. He hesitated at the top.

"In the water," said Ableson.

He glared at the Almighty and jumped into the tank, clinging to the side, his arms and head over the top.

"All the way to the bottom."

He barked his displeasure but dropped to the bottom. He'd kill Ableson if anything happened to Sweet.

The Almighty's hands trembled as he opened the door. He glanced at the tank and then began examining Sweet. He withdrew blood and then backed out of the cage, shutting the door. "Stay in the tank."

Ableson studied her blood under the microscope, his pale face growing whiter. Sweet trembled and moaned on the ground.

"It's happening. There is nothing I can do," said Ableson.

Mutter had drifted to the top and clung to the side. He slapped his arm with his flipper. They had given him a shot and it had made him better for a little while.

"What? No, I can't give her more serum. We've gone too fast as it is."

He slapped his arm again.

"I don't understand," said Ableson. "She understands you, not me." He walked back to the cage. "We could try slowing it down. I could try the stabilizer."

Mutter grunted, nodding his head.

Ableson looked at the blood under the microscope again, mumbling to himself, "She's further along than you were. The dose might have been too strong or the serum could metabolize differently in Servants."

Ableson left the room and came back a few minutes later. Mutter had climbed out of the tank and was on his way toward Sweet.

"Get back in the water. I'll give her the stabilizer." He waved a syringe in the air.

Mutter hopped back into the tank and waited while Ableson opened the door and injected the medicine into Sweet. She cried out.

Ableson's eyes flew to Mutter. "Stay or I leave."

He slapped his tail from side-to-side, but otherwise didn't move.

Sweet began to tremble violently. Ableson held her down, his white skin paling even more as Sweet's entire body shook and then fell still. He glanced at the tank as he backed out of the enclosure.

Mutter popped his head out of the water and grunted.

"I...I'm sorry." Ableson hurried out of the room.

Something was wrong. He jumped out of the tank and raced to Sweet's side, pulling her into his arms. He almost sighed in relief. Her fever was fading. She'd be okay. He brushed the hair away from her face. She was pale and still, a hint of blue around her lips. His mother had been blue when she'd...the breath froze in his lungs. He placed his flipper over her heart. There was no beat, no pulse, no life. This couldn't be. It wasn't possible. He shook her, grunting and moaning. She flopped in his arms like a doll, boneless and loose. She had left him. He roared as he pulled her onto his lap, rocking back and forth.

He was still sitting there when Ableson returned.

"I'm...I'm sorry. Truly I am." He walked toward the

enclosure. "We were too aggressive with the serum. She was so small; her body couldn't handle it."

Mutter didn't bother to look at the Almighty. He couldn't get out of the cage to kill him so there was no point in paying any attention to him.

They sat in silence most of the night. His skin itched from being out of the water, but he would not let her go. He'd left her alone all day while she was in pain and dying; he wouldn't leave her again.

Ableson stood. "Look, I hate to do this, but I have to get her out of here before the professor comes back." He moved to the cage. "He can't find out what we did."

We? Mutter wanted to laugh but his vocals didn't work like that anymore, so he ignored the Almighty. He no longer cared what they wanted. There was nothing they could do to him now.

"Please go back into the water and let me take her. I'll give her a proper burial. I promise."

Mutter didn't move.

"Please, don't make this harder than it has to be." A few minutes later, Ableson left.

Whispers from down the hallway slipped into the room. Ableson and two of the Guards approached.

"So, once we dart him, what do we do with the body?" asked Laddie.

"Take it to the secondary facility. I need to examine her to see what went wrong," said Ableson.

Mutter stood and carried her to the tank. He kissed her and then released her into the water. She floated on the top. He jumped in after her, cradling her in his arms as he submerged. Tiny bubbles trickled from between her lips and out of her nose. He placed his mouth over her face, catching her last breath.

The door opened.

"Where is he?" asked Jorge.

Ableson hurried to the cage. "He was sitting right here." His eyes searched the enclosure and then drifted to the tank. "Shit. He must be in the water."

"Where's the Servant?" asked Jorge.

"With him, I'm sure," said Ableson.

"That's not good," said the Laddie.

"You'll have to shoot him," said Ableson.

"Not without dr—"

"Shut up." Ableson nodded toward the tank.

"You've seen the way those things can leap out of the water," continued Laddie. "There's no place I can stand that is close enough to shoot him and still far enough away that he can't get me."

"Shit, shit, shit." Ableson began to pace. "How are we going to get her?"

"Get who?" asked the professor as he entered the room.

"You're early." Ableson's voice was accusing.

"I didn't realize that I was supposed to follow your schedule in my lab."

"No. Of course not. I'm sorry." Sweat trickled down Ableson's cheek.

"What are the Guards doing here with the gun? I thought we decided to wait to have the tank drained."

"Yes, we did." Ableson paused, his eyes darting around and then they widened. "I have bad news. He finally turned on the Servant, just as you expected."

Rage flared through Mutter's pain. The Almighty was blaming him for this. He pulled her closer, stroking her hair.

Conguise stared at the tank. "Well, it was to be expected. Once they reach this stage, they are wild, intent only on their own survival." He walked to the chair and sat. "What are you waiting for?"

The two Guards looked at Ableson.

"Ah, well, we might not be able to"—Ableson nodded at the tank—"he might not be hungry."

"Then let him feed. We can observe him from the top again and clean the tank in a day or so."

The Guards left and Ableson gathered his notepad and headed for the door.

"Where did he attack her? At the edge of the tank or on land?" asked the professor.

"Ah...tank."

The professor studied him closely. "You are not a very good liar, never have been. That makes you a perfect assistant."

"I was asleep. I didn't see anything." Ableson's face reddened.

The professor frowned. "What did you hear?"

"Nothing. Not really."

"No scream? No splash?"

Ableson shook his head still staring at the tank.

Mutter let go of Sweet. Ableson was not going to get away with this. He hit the tank hard and fast. Ableson staggered backward, stumbling into the table. The professor jumped from his seat. Mutter hit the tank again.

"Seems he's a bit upset," said the professor.

"He loved her," said Ableson.

Mutter hit the tank again.

"Loved? I don't believe the other classes have that capability, but maybe...no. He's just upset that he killed his mate. It's interesting that even though his instincts overrode his prior feelings, they still lurk inside of him." The professor moved so that he stood right in front of where Mutter hit the wall of the tank over and over again. "We may need to remove her body. I would assume that he'd eat her, but...he's very upset. Can't have him breaking the glass can we? If he does that, he'll have to be euthanized and I think we can still learn a lot from this one."

"We...we can try and feed him," said Ableson.

"Yes, if he's this upset he probably hasn't eaten her, not much of her anyway."

CHAPTER 14

A HOUSE SERVANT HUNG over the top of the tank. Mutter was hungry and exhausted. As soon as Ableson had left to get the Guards, he'd stopped slamming into the wall and had gathered Sweet from the bottom, cuddling her close. His stomach rumbled. He stared up at the Servant and then gently placed Sweet on the floor of the tank. He swam upward, jumping and grabbing the old male in his arms. He hit the water, twisted and spun for a second. The Servant never struggled. He began to feed, but the blood was bitter. He let the Servant go. It hung in the water, not floating and not sinking. He retrieved Sweet. Maybe, he'd quit eating. He'd die and then be with her once again. His stomach clenched and his vision began to blur. His head bobbed. Voices tickled his sleep. Light assaulted his eyes but that was impossible. The water was murky, no light allowed to enter. He forced his eyes open.

"Get him out now, we don't want him to drown like the other one," said the professor.

The Almightys knew nothing. He slept in the water all the

time. A rope drifted near his face. His eyes followed it upward. Two Guards stood at the edge of the tank. Scar held a search light which was pointing down at him. She directed Jorge who lowered the rope.

Mutter grabbed the line and yanked. Jorge screamed as he fell into the water. Mutter burst into the air, knocking Scar into the tank on his way out. Conguise and Ableson stood on the floor near the stairs, staring up at him, their faces whiter than white. The professor was the first to turn and race to the cage door. Ableson was only a few seconds behind, but it was enough. Mutter was faster than they'd thought. He'd grown accustomed to his new feet and how to maneuver on land. He tackled Ableson, slamming the Almighty's head into the concrete. Blood pooled under Ableson's skull, but it wasn't enough. He would tear the Almighty apart. He grabbed Ableson's arm and twisted until the limb tore from the torso. There was a slight pinch on his chest and his vision blurred as he looked up. Conguise stood in front of him, gun in hand.

The roar of rushing water was the first thing that registered with Mutter as he forced his eyes open. He liked the sound, but something poked at the edge of his conscience that this was bad, not comforting. He was lying on his back, concrete under him, cold and hard. There were bars all around, close, not like before. He turned on his side, his vision still fuzzy and his head groggy. Water swirled down the drain in the floor. Dirty water. His heart picked up pace. His water. His home. He rolled over and pushed himself to his knees.

"He's awake." Jorge held the hose attached to the tank, aiming it at the drain in the floor.

"Hmm," grunted Scar as she lifted a sack.

"You should get"—Jorge nodded toward another sack—"that out of here before he realizes..."

Laddie hefted the other bag over his shoulder, groaning a bit. "Heavier than she looked."

Mutter's eyes flew to Laddie. The sack was oblong and the same size as a small Servant. He tried to yell "No" but all that came out was a strangled bark. He was too unsteady to stand so he crawled to the side of the cage closest to Laddie, reaching through the bars and barking his shrill cry, pleading.

"Too late. He knows." The hose wobbled in Jorge's hands.

"He doesn't know anything." Scar headed toward the door.

"This ain't right." Laddie stared at Mutter and their eyes locked.

"Laddie, come on," said Scar. "It don't matter if it's right or not. We have to do what we're ordered." She glanced out the door. "Hurry before they come back."

"It ain't right," repeated Laddie as he walked toward Mutter.

"Don't," warned Scar.

"Keep watch," said Jorge. "Let Laddie do this. This...thing was a Guard just like us."

"Yeah. Well, if we get caught we might take this thing's place." Scar glanced down the hallway. "Just hurry up."

Laddie knelt near the cage, placing the sack on the ground. Mutter strained but still couldn't reach. He grunted, eyes pleading with the Guard to understand and to move her closer. He waved his flipper.

"Don't let him get ahold of her," said Scar.

"Oh, Scar, you worry too much," said Jorge. "Let him touch her Laddie. What's it going to hurt?"

"If we can't get her away from him—"

"I'm not an idiot, Scar. I won't let him grab her." Laddie pulled the cloth down exposing Sweet's face and shifting her a bit closer to the cage.

Mutter grunted again, pressing harder into the bars. He needed her. She was his. Laddie moved the body a little more. She wasn't close enough for Mutter to grasp and pull close like he wanted, but it was the best he was going to get. He hummed as he stroked her hair. They would take her soon; there was nothing he could do about that. Her pale green eyes were cloudy but they called to him. *Stay with me. We belong together.*

"They're coming," whispered Scar.

"Sorry." Laddie shifted Sweet's body away and covered her with the sack. He stood and hefted her over his shoulder. "Sorry," he said again as he headed toward the door.

Mutter pulled his arm back into the cage as Conguise walked into the room.

"Is that the last of it?" asked Conguise.

Mutter's lip twitched. She was not an "it".

"Yes, Professor," said Scar. "The section is almost full."

"Already?"

"The Aranea18 incident left—"

"Of course. Flush it before we clean his tank again." He faced Mutter. "We should never have let the water get that dirty." Conguise pulled out his notepad. "Surprised that he's awake. His metabolism is fast. I'll increase the sedative but we have to devise a better way to deliver it. I don't want him to drown."

Laddie shifted the sack on his shoulder. "Sir, a top on that tank would do the trick. We could drain the water halfway and then shoot him. He wouldn't be able to jump out of the tank..."

Conguise turned to face the Guard. "A top? That will never work." He studied the tank and then scribbled in his notepad.

"Of course, sorry." Laddie followed Scar out the door. She purposely rammed his shoulder with hers as they left the room.

Mutter turned back to watch the remaining water wash down the drain. Sweet would be dumped in the sewer where rats and bugs could eat her. She'd be alone again. She hated being alone.

Soon, the tank was drained and House Servants were sent inside to clean it. Then it was refilled. When it was almost full Laddie and Scar returned. Laddie held a gun.

Conguise handed Laddie a dart. "I increased the dosage. He'll be out the rest of the evening. Remove the small cage."

"What do you want done with him?" asked Laddie.

"Leave him there. When he wakes he'll go back to the tank." Conguise headed for the door.

"Food?" asked Laddie.

"He seems sad. Don't feed him until the day after tomorrow. A little hunger should go a long way in curing his depression." Conguise left the room.

Laddie approached the cage. Jorge and Scar were shoving the rolled up hose it into one of the closets outside of the large enclosure.

"Sorry about this." Laddie raised the gun.

Mutter looked away. It didn't matter what they did to him

any longer. There was a sharp pinch on his shoulder but he didn't bother to knock the needle out. He just waited for the blackness to bury his pain.

Mutter awoke to quiet. No talking, no breathing, just the hum of the lights. He sat up, his head spinning. He was alone, completely alone. No Almighty sat observing him, or sleeping in the chair. No Guards were in the room. He pulled the dart from his shoulder. His head pounded and his skin itched. He'd been out of the water too long. Memories flooded back into his drugged brain. They'd taken her from him again. He crawled toward the tank, his insides hollow and aching. He leaned against the glass, staring at the path the water had taken. She was down there somewhere, but at least she was free. She'd escaped just like she'd said she would. He sat up. He could go too. He could find her.

He dropped into the water and floated for a few minutes to refresh his dry skin and then he went to where Sweet had hidden the bone. He carried it to the drain in the floor. It took some time to maneuver the bone in his flippers without losing it down the drain but eventually, he was able to unfasten the screws and lift the lid. He took one final dip in the water to remoisten his skin and then he squeezed into the pipe. It was a tight fit but he was slippery and the path was almost straight down. There was one turn where he got stuck but he wriggled and squirmed and someone flushed a toilet or ran water somewhere because it rushed up to him, seeping around him and helping to push him forward. He skidded down the pipe on the remnants of the water and plopped into the sewer.

It was dark, dank and smelly. Mold grew on the walls and

things scurried past his feet, but he ignored them. He had to find her. He searched tunnel after tunnel. He had no idea of how much time had passed. It was all one endless nightmare of foul odor and darkness but then she was there, lying on a pile of bones. Rats and small crabs crawled on her skin, feeding.

He roared, racing to her. He stumbled, fell to his knees and crawled the rest of the way, snapping at any creature that dared come near him. Her eyes were almost white now, but they were still green in his memory. He pulled her close, stroking her hair. His vocal cords trembled but he forced a few final words for her. "W..eet. Lo...ve."

He cradled her close to his chest as he began searching for an exit. Hours passed, maybe days, but he kept walking, trying to locate a hint of fresh air that would lead out. He'd catch a whiff every now and then and would adjust his path. His body ached from carrying her, but he continued moving. He would never leave her again. A roar echoed in the tunnels. He stilled. Water. A lot of water. That much would hit him hard.

He ducked into another tunnel, but the sound was the same. They were flushing the system. Water was coming at him from all directions. He had to find an exit or somewhere to wait out the rush. He wouldn't drown, but he could get smashed against the walls. He ran, breathing deeply, praying for a trace of fresh air to point him in the right direction and then there it was, just a little, but enough. He pushed himself to run faster. The roar was closer now, the spray of water at his back. The weight of Sweet slowed him down but he would not drop her, not even to save himself. The first wave knocked his legs out from under him. The second blast carried him along, tossing him about. He clung to Sweet as he hit the side of the tunnel and then tumbled and hit the roof. He was spun about like one of his prey and then he slammed into something and darkness swept over him.

When he came to, he was lying on his stomach in a small culvert half-submerged in water. His arms were still wrapped around Sweet. He sat up, coughing. Remnants of the sewer's trash filled his gills. He used the tip of his flipper to pry it free. Once he could breathe he pulled Sweet close. The Almightys had flushed the system, trying to kill him. Instead, they had set him free, him and Sweet. Now, he'd take her home. He tucked her under his arm, slipping into the water. He moved from culvert to culvert until he found his way into a small stream. It led to the river and that took him to the Lake of Sins.

He placed her in the high grass on the bank and dove under the calm water, searching the hidden crevices and tunnels of the lake for a place that Sweet would like. He settled on a small alcove under the island. He swam to shore and searched the woods, gathering branches and carrying them to the underwater cave.

Once he was done assembling her home, he surfaced and froze. A fox had its face buried in her chest, feeding. He wanted to roar and send it fleeing, but his instincts warred with his temper. He slipped under the water, moving closer. The fox was wary, sensing danger. It kept looking back at land, never suspecting that the danger was only a few feet away, lurking below. He swam a little closer and then jumped from the water. His flippers snatched at the fox but the animal was fast and its fur made it slippery. It let out a yelp, Sweet's rib bone dropping from its jaws. It raced off into the woods, tail between its legs. He bellowed his rage, but the fox was gone, his dinner gone. He picked up her rib bone, placing it back into her chest and carried her to her new home. He placed her into the crevice, tangling her in the branches. Once she was secure, weariness seeped into his body, making his bones heavy. He held her hand and slept.

A slight ripple in the water stirred him from his rest. There were small fish darting around Sweet, feeding on her. He snapped at them, gobbling up as many as he could catch as he chased them away. He returned to find more nibbling on her eyes and chest. He'd never win. They would eat her until there was nothing left, or he could keep her with him, always a part of him. He kissed her cold lips and then buried his face in her stomach and fed.

He ate until he was full. Then he slept and fed again, until she was no more. All that remained were her bones. He tucked them into the alcove. They'd be safe now. There was nothing left that anything would want and she would be a part of him forever. He placed his flipper on her pile of bones, closing his eyes and remembering every day they'd had together and imagining every day they should have had. He'd rest for a while, gain strength and learn how to catch prey.

Sweet understood. He saw it in her face when he shut his eyes, but he'd made her a promise and one day, he'd leave. He'd learn the forest and the hidden passages that led into the city from the Lake of Sins. Eventually, he'd find the one that would lead to Conguise's lab. It would take time, there were many tunnels but he had nothing else but time....and hatred.

Thanks for reading *Conguise Chronicles: Rise of the River Man*. I hope you enjoyed the story.

If you liked the story, please leave a review on Amazon or any of the other ebook vendors. You can find the links on my website: www.lsodea.com

If you haven't done so already
GET YOUR FREE
ELECTRONIC COPY OF LAKE OF SINS: SECRETS IN BLOOD
HTTP://LSODEA.COM/DOWNLOAD-SECRETS-IN-BLOOD/

OR GO TO MY WEBSITE: http://www.lsodea.com

If you already have the ebook or prefer physical books (I'm just getting used to reading ebooks myself ☺), you can still signup with my Readers' Group. I sponsor giveaways which often include physical copies of my books and other promotions.

HTTP://LSODEA.COM/JOIN-THE-LAKE-OF-

SINS-READERS-GROUP/

Also, check out the sneak peek at the first book in the Lake of Sins Series – Escape (which is also free for a limited time) right after the Characters section on the next page.

CHARACTERS

Ableson: A male Almighty in his thirties with blond hair. He is an assistant to Professor Conguise.

Almightys: The ruling class. They are between five and six feet tall. Generally, have dark hair and white skin.

Araldo: Their god.

Aranea18: One of Professor Conguise's projects. Spider-like creature.

Anna: The Almighty girl who owned Sweet.

Great Death: The event that swept over the earth, killing most humans, all domestic animals and all wild animals larger than a wild turkey.

Guards: Belong to the Almightys. They hunt for the Almightys and protect the Almightys. They vary in size and hair color. Their eyes are usually brown. They have large canine teeth and an enhanced sense of smell and hearing. The males generally wear facial hair.

House Servants: Belong to Almightys. They manage the households and businesses of the Almightys. They are slender in build and short, between four and five feet tall. They have fangs and claws and their eyes are a vibrant hue. They have an enhanced sense of smell and hearing.

Jorge: A male Guard. Belongs to Professor Conguise.

Laddie: A male Guard. Belongs to Professor Conguise.

Mutter: A Guard. Used to belong to Vickers and was used as a fighter. He is big and scarred.

Noodles: A Guard who is involved in the black market.

Parson: An Almighty who works with Professor Conguise.

Professor Conguise: A male Almighty in his late fifties. He's tall and thin with gray hair. Runs the lab where Mutter is taken.

Satcha: A male House Servant. Runs the Guards' Shelter where Mutter is held.

Scar: A female Guard. Belongs to Professor Conguise.

Sovee: A Guard, owned by Vickers. He is a retired fighter who now trains the fighters for Vickers.

Sweet: A small, female House Servant who lives at the grocer's.

River-People: Fish-like creatures. Can live in or out of water, but prefer to be in the water. They can breathe both above and below water. They have scales for skin, sharp teeth. Hunt from below the water and drag their prey under to drown it.

Tantiori: An Almighty who works with Professor Conguise.

Truent: An Almighty who works with Professor Conguise.

Vickers: A male Almighty. Uses Guards to fight.

Voice, the: A creature, former Guard, in the lab at the same time as Mutter.

Feeding Fersia – Volume Two in the Conguise Chronicles Series

CHAPTER 1: McBrid

MCBRID RACED OUT OF his office and down the hallway, following the faint sound of the muffled scream. He should stop. Go back, but his legs kept moving. He should've never heard the noise, but he had and he knew that voice. It was Charlie. The damn Guard was too young to be in a place like this but here he was and he was in trouble.

A House Servant shoved past him, barely limping on a leg that'd been broken too badly to repair. Apparently, when monstrous death stares someone in the face, injuries cease to exist.

McBrid didn't hesitate at the door. He should've. Any sane Almighty would've, but there was the problem. He wasn't pure Almighty. Thirty-two years of hiding the Guard in him, ruined over one garbled scream of terror. He burst into the room.

Charlie was on the floor, several feet over the line that separated safety from death. The young Guard was trying to scramble away from Aranea18, the giant spider mutation, who had one of her four, long, hairy legs wrapped around his waist. The two claws on the end kept him in place but didn't dig into his flesh. That pleasure would be saved for her fangs.

"Help me," yelled Charlie. "Please! Help me." He clawed at the tile but Aranea18 dragged him closer to her, closer to death.

The other Guard McBrid had assigned to feed Aranea18 with Charlie, was on the floor near the cage. He had no idea why she wasn't eating him. One of her other legs wrapped around Charlie's face, sliding into his mouth and silencing his screams. He bit down and she screeched, letting him go for one quick instant. As the Guard lunged forward, McBrid grabbed his hand, pulling Charlie toward him, but Aranea18 wasn't going to be denied her meal. She grabbed Charlie's ankles with two of her good legs, flailing the injured one in the air as if chastising them and clinging to the bar of the cage with her other leg.

"Don't let go," whispered Charlie, his big, brown eyes wide with fear.

McBrid tightened his grip but he was no match for Aranea18. He slid forward with the young Guard. He tugged and scrambled backward but the Aranea was strong and hungry, her fangs snapping together as poison dripped down her furry torso. In another moment he'd be over that line too. She looked at him, with her eight, black eyes, four on top and four on bottom, and let go of Charlie with one of her legs. She reached for McBrid's arm. He dropped his hold and scooted away from the line, away from death. He hadn't planned on letting go, he hadn't meant to but instinct had kicked in and this one was probably Almighty not Guard.

"No, please," yelled Charlie, his eyes almost popping from his head as he clawed at the tile trying to get away.

McBrid shouldn't do anything. Guards' lives didn't matter. They were expendable, easily replaced. He'd heard it his entire life and he hated the truth in the words as much as the lie. To him and his mother Guards had never been replaceable.

The poles they used to control the Araneas were lying next to the cage. He jumped to his feet, ran across the lab and grabbed the hose used to clean the enclosures. He unraveled it from the wheel and ran toward Charlie, stopping right at the line. He turned it on, aiming for Aranea18. The water burst forward, hitting her in the head. She screamed but tightened her leg around Charlie's ankle. She wasn't one to give up easily. He lowered his aim to her abdomen. She was sensitive there. She flew backward hitting the wall of the cage. This time, the sound she made—a grating, screeching cacophony of pain and anger—echoed through his bones almost causing him to piss his pants. Then, she dropped to the floor, falling silent.

Charlie scrambled to the door, as McBrid turned off the hose. His heart hammered in his chest as he stared at the Aranea. Her legs twitched and then curled inward as if protecting herself.

"You okay?" he asked.

Charlie nodded and then bent over and vomited.

He wanted to puke too. Aranea18 wasn't moving. She was the most important creature in Professor Conguise's lab and he was pretty sure he'd just killed her to save a Guard.

Other Books By L. S. O'Dea

Book 1 of the Lake of Sins series.
Free for a limited time in ebook format.

CHAPTER 1

TRINITY BRUSHED THE DIRT OFF HER HANDS and stretched, exposing her claws and giving the small of her back a good scratch. She was the last to finish preparing her fields for winter. Everyone else was gone, hiding in their huts. Producers did not like the night, but being half House Servant she didn't mind it. When she was alone or in the dark, she didn't have to hide her claws or fangs. Still, she retracted her nails as she bent to pick up the spade and hand trowel. It was habit now. She'd learned as a child that either she concealed her differences or her parents would. She ran her tongue over her large sharp canines, so different from the Producers' flat teeth. Mom and Dad had filed her fangs down only a couple of times before she'd learned to smile with her lips closed.

She tucked the tools under her arms and took a moment to memorize this view of her home. The Producer village sat in a valley. On the north and where she stood in the west were the fields, fallow now and waiting for winter. Dirt trails ran down the hill and into the camp, most leading to the pine cabins huddled together in the center of town with fires burning in pyres outside each hut. A few paths broke free and escaped to the edge of town where smaller, older cottages like hers sat. Other trails led to Shadow Lake, fed from the Elavital River which flowed from the thick, lush forest on the south and east side of the valley.

She sighed and headed down a trail toward home. She'd miss the freedom of the forest once she was gone. Although, it wasn't as much fun sneaking into the woods alone as it had been with Travis. The two of them used to talk about what the earth might have been like before the Great Death brought extinction to all animals larger than twenty pounds and death to most humans. She'd learned about the event in some of the books that her dad had borrowed from his master's house. Producers weren't supposed to read, but Dad had taught her and her mom. According to one book, the Almightys were the last descendants of the human race. She'd searched every book she had but there was no mention of the ancestry of the other classes.

She stopped at the storage shed and put her tools away. She wouldn't need them again, ever. Within a couple of weeks, she'd be taken just like Travis had been last year. She turned onto the path that led through town. There was no doubt in her mind that her name would be on the Harvest List. The Almightys only chose the finest examples of Producers to stay and breed. The males were always the tallest and strongest, averaging seven to eight feet in height and almost as wide. The females were at least six-feet tall and had to have large, wide hips and big breasts. She glanced down at her less-than-curvy shape. After the Terrible Sickness had killed her brothers and sisters nine years ago, her mom had switched her name with her younger sister, hoping to give her time to fill out. That hadn't happened. At almost seventeen, she was over three years older than the other girls up for the Harvest List but still only five foot eight and less endowed. She shook her head. She was definitely a Lister.

"Hey, look who it is," Clarabelle said, shoving Randy toward her.

Clarabelle and her group of friends stood near some huts along the path. She groaned, glancing down at her filthy clothes. It was just her luck that Randy would see her like this. If she hadn't been so tired she might have remembered that the teenagers who were up for the Harvest List often hung around outside the huts well into the night. Sometimes, they even mated with each other. It was forbidden but the Lead Producers didn't enforce the rule; they too had once been teenage Producers dreading their List year.

She stopped. Experience had taught her that it was easier to let Clarabelle have her say. She kept her eyes down. She made the others nervous when she stared at them. It had something to do with her not blinking enough. It was one more gift from her House Servant father.

Clarabelle stepped up alongside Randy so that the two of them blocked her path. Well, they thought that they did. She could zip around them in a flash. She'd love to do it too, but she wasn't allowed. Producers weren't slow, but it took them awhile to get going, unlike her.

"Have you finished my fields?" Clarabelle asked.

"What do you mean by that?" She glanced up at the other girl, her eyes narrowing. Her fields were the best yielding; they had to be in order for her and her mom to survive. The first five acres that a family farmed, the Almightys took ninety-five percent of the output. The percentage went down every five acres but not by much.

"Oh, you poor thing. You don't know." Clarabelle feigned sympathy.

"Know what?" she asked in a bored tone. Now, Clarabelle would tease her about being on the Harvest List, like she didn't know that already. She wasn't blind or stupid.

"Your mother is going to be retired this year and it's obvious that you're a Lister." Clarabelle quit trying to look sad, her eyes gleaming.

She raised her head and stared directly at the other girl. Her mom wasn't that old. There was no way that she was being retired. She clenched her jaw, trying to calm herself. She didn't care what Clarabelle thought of her, but many of the others would be taken with her. She didn't want them to have any reason to hate her once Clarabelle was out of the picture. She took a deep breath. "The Retirement List hasn't been read yet." *That actually sounded pleasant.*

She stepped aside and started to walk away but Clarabelle

blocked her path. That was it. That one simple motion and her temper flared to life. "Neither has the Harvest List. You may not get to stay. Mirabelle didn't." As soon as the words were out of her mouth she froze. She'd gone too far. Mirabelle was the first one in Clarabelle's family to make the List.

"How dare you, freak." Clarabelle shoved her. "Don't ever say my sister's name again."

She flinched. They called her names behind her back, but never to her face. It hurt more for some reason.

"Do you hear me, freak?" Clarabelle shoved her again and she stumbled backward.

She was either going to cry or strike back; she refused to cry. "Mirabelle. Mirabelle was taken. Mirabelle has one leg shorter than the other."

The others gasped. No one spoke about the deformity.

Her hands curled into fists at her sides. Clarabelle's face paled and then turned a raging red. This was not a good sign. The others moved in, surrounding her. She glanced around, looking for an opening. There was none. She was going to get it now. She couldn't even defend herself for fear of her claws or teeth being seen. If that happened, her mom and Remy would be in trouble too.

"Hey, you kids. Break it up," shouted an adult male.

The group of Producers eased back a little. She exhaled in relief. Troy was heading their way.

Clarabelle grabbed her arm, tight. "By this time next year, I'll be eating crops grown from your soil and nursing Stuart's baby and you'll be gone. I hope they have something horrible planned for you."

Randy's jaw tightened at the mention of Stuart. He shot

Clarabelle an angry, desperate look and walked away.

She jerked free from Clarabelle's hold. It wasn't fair. Stuart was Travis's brother. He deserved better than Clarabelle. "Stuart will hate you before long. Your big boobs and fat butt won't keep him happy not when you're so mean and nasty."

"Back up, back up." Troy pushed through the group, using his club instead of his hand. "What's going on here? Trinity? Clarabelle?"

The hatred and anger slid off Clarabelle's features as she turned toward Troy. She shook her head, making her long hair flow.

Trinity choked back a laugh. Clarabelle's charms wouldn't work on Troy but his attraction to other males was a well-guarded secret.

"She was teasing me about"—Clarabelle wiped at her eyes—"Mirabelle."

"Is that true?" Troy turned toward her, frowning.

"Not..."

"Yes," replied a female from the group.

The worst part was that she did feel bad about bringing up Mirabelle. The other girl had been nice to her. Mirabelle hadn't been a friend, but she had been a kind face in the crowd. "It wasn't like that. I mean..."

"It wasn't nice," said Troy. "Tell her you're sorry."

She looked up at him. He wasn't kidding. He was a Lead Producer. She had to obey but not without a fight. "She said my mother is being retired and I'm a Lister."

Troy's face softened. He smiled at her as if she amused him. "It sounds like you should apologize to each other."

Her eyes met Clarabelle's. For once they were in

agreement. That was not going to happen.

"I don't want her apology," Clarabelle said.

"That's fine, but Trinity may still want yours." Troy's eyes narrowed.

"You can't be serious?" Clarabelle's face was ashen.

"Oh, but I am," said Troy.

She tried not to smile but couldn't quite stop her lips from turning up at the corners. This was a dream come true. Sometimes, she really loved Troy. He understood her. He'd been born poor and had risen to the ranks of Lead Producer. He didn't care for Clarabelle's family any more than she did, but he did demand respect. Clarabelle was truly caught now.

"Trinity, do you want an apology?"

She inhaled, savoring the moment. If she went through with this, Clarabelle would get her revenge. The smart thing would be to say that she didn't want the apology, but she did. Oh, how she did. She straightened and met Clarabelle's glare. "Yes, I do."

"I will get you for this," Clarabelle said under her breath.

"That sounded like a threat," Troy said.

Clarabelle's face whitened. Threats were not tolerated. In reality they happened all the time, but no one was stupid enough to issue one right in front of a Lead Producer.

"I'm sorry, Troy. I didn't mean it."

"Apologize to Trinity," he said.

"Sorry," snapped Clarabelle.

"That didn't sound sincere." Troy smirked.

Clarabelle exhaled through her teeth, making a noise like a hissing snake. "I'm sorry, Trinity."

It was the worst apology she'd ever heard.

"Do you accept?" asked Troy, his eyes bright with amusement.

She'd love to make Clarabelle say it again, but as it was, she was going to have to hide in her house for a few days, maybe weeks. Clarabelle would be watching for any opportunity to seek revenge. "Yes. It's fine."

Troy clapped his hands. "Well, that's done then. All of you need to head home. I won't be patrolling again tonight."

Was that a warning to her, or a message to the others that they could sneak off together without being caught? She couldn't tell by his face.

"Trinity, I'm going your way. Let me see you home," he said.

She nodded, relieved. Her house sat on the outskirts of the encampment. She didn't think Clarabelle would come after her tonight, but she wasn't positive. They headed toward her home, walking in silence. The quiet seemed to unnerve him.

"You shouldn't let yourself get caught up by that group. They could hurt you. Rem...your father would kill me if anything happened to you."

"I know. It won't happen again. Thanks for...well, saving me."

He patted her shoulder. "No problem. Why were you out so late? Working the fields?"

She was covered in dirt. What did he think she'd been doing? But he'd been nice to her and Remy would be mad if she were snotty. "Yeah."

The automated light hummed to life, illuminating part of the perimeter and the area right outside the encampment. It penetrated a bit into the forest, but not much, the vegetation was too dense.

"Looks like I'm going to be late for work," he said, more to himself than her.

The guard shack was only a few yards away. It was Troy's first evening on duty in a month, so he and Remy would spend most of the night together. The Almightys were very strict about same-sex mating. If Troy and Remy were caught, they would be publicly executed. She prayed that wouldn't happen. Remy was like a father to her. Actually, he was supposed to be her father. He was her mother's assigned mate and in a lot of ways was a better dad than her real one. At least he was around.

"You don't have to walk me all the way home," she said.

"Are you sure?" Excitement shone in his eyes.

It wasn't too far to her house, but between here and there was the maze. All the crops that were harvested were packed in wooden boxes, waiting to be carted away by Benedictine's, the Almighty who ran their encampment, Guards and distributed to the other classes. There were hundreds of crates, stacked several feet high. Once you were in the maze, you couldn't be seen from the outside. It was a bit spooky in the dark, but she'd hurry through them. "I'll be fine."

Troy patted her shoulder again and hurried to the guard shack. She took a deep breath and darted into the maze. She was about halfway through when Randy stepped out of the shadows. Her heart picked up pace as she looked for an escape. She was boxed in, the large crates essentially making a hallway. Her only options were to go back or to go past him.

"Don't be scared," he said.

She hesitated. She wasn't sure why, but there was

something in his tone that reminded her of the old Randy, the little boy who had been her first friend.

At five, Randy had caught an inflammation of the lungs and the other Producers' parents refused to let their offspring near him. Her mom was a healer so he was at their house a lot. He had been a quiet, kind boy often helping her to find and care for injured animals. A few years later he was healthy and he grew, fast. He started hanging around with the other kids and forgot about her, but she'd never forgotten about him.

Randy moved closer. If he reached out he could touch her. She took a step back.

He stopped. "Sorry about earlier." He lowered his gaze. "Sometimes when I'm around Clarabelle, I do things..." He shrugged, giving her a shy smile.

Why was he being nice to her? Usually, he ignored her.

"We're all a little nervous about the announcement. My family has a fifty percent List rate."

This was more like Randy, always thinking about himself. Her family had a one hundred percent List rate.

"I'm sorry. I mean, fifty percent must sound pretty good to you." His shoulders sagged.

She glared at him. It was true, but he didn't need to point it out. His brown eyes were soft and sad. Maybe, he hadn't meant it to be mean. The announcement did put everyone on edge.

"Clarabelle shouldn't have said what she did about your mom."

"Thank you." She studied him.

He smiled, his teeth a quick flash of white in the darkness. "I was worried that you'd refuse to talk to me. I wouldn't blame you. Not after the way I've treated you." He glanced around. "It's really dark. I can barely see you."

He took a couple of steps forward; she didn't move back.

"Do you remember Chirps? I swear I still see him around sometimes."

She smiled. Chirps had been a baby crow that had lost its parents. They'd raised him, years ago. "I see him, especially in the spring."

He gently touched her cheek, his fingers rough from working the fields. "You're pretty dirty," he said, a smile in his tone.

"Yeah." Really, what else was there to say?

"You have the most gorgeous eyes." He ran his thumb over her cheek.

She stiffened. Her physical appearance was a sore subject for her. She was almost a perfect blend of both House Servant and Producer which meant she didn't belong with either class. Her features weren't as delicate as a House Servant's or as strong as a Producer's. Her nose was either too large or not big enough and her eyes were the wrong color. House Servants' eyes varied in hues but they were always vibrant, never a dull brown like a Producer's. Hers were neither vibrant nor brown; they were gold. "Everyone hates my eyes. You tell..."

"That's because Clarabelle is jealous."

She turned her face away and he dropped his hand. Was that true? Did Clarabelle hate her because she was jealous? More important, did he really like her eyes?

He reached out again, but this time he grasped a strand of her hair that had come free from the band that held it back. "She especially hates your hair. I wish there was light so I could see the other colors. It's beautiful with the reds and gold mixed in with the brown." He pulled her hairband down, freeing her long locks. "Beautiful. So, soft."

She should step away. He'd ignored her all these years, but she'd liked him for so long. Was it that impossible to believe that he might like her too? They had been best friends once.

He moved a little closer. Was he going to kiss her? She waited. His breath intermingled with hers.

"I don't want to be taken," he said.

"Me either." That was the expected reply and she meant it, kind of. If she could have someone here, someone for her, then she'd like to stay, but if everyone were going to continue to hate her then maybe being taken would be better, leaving certainly would be.

"A lot of the others have been...mating. You know. I mean, I may never get to try it if I'm taken. Even if I stay, I may be assigned to some gross, old Producer and never get to do it with someone I like." His hand moved from her hair to her neck, massaging gently.

She stiffened a bit. Did she want this? It might be her only chance too.

"Don't be afraid," he whispered. "No one really cares if we do this."

He was right. Even if a Lead Producer caught them, there wasn't much of a punishment. As long as it was close to the time of the reading of the Harvest List, they'd pass off any pregnancies as the product of the assigned mating. The problem was that she wasn't sure that she wanted to do this with him. She liked him, a lot, but she didn't trust him. Too many years had passed since they'd been friends. Still, she didn't want to this moment to end.

He pulled her closer. She could feel the warmth of his skin through his shirt. He lowered his head. This was her first kiss. His lips were warm and soft. It was nice. She ran her hands up his chest and around his neck, leaning into him. He groaned and ran his tongue across her bottom lip. *That's weird*. She tried to pull away but he held her tight.

"Relax. You'll like it. I promise."

What did he mean by that? The females never discussed this with their offspring until they were assigned a mate. Maybe, it was only the daughters who were kept in the dark about mating. Randy seemed to know what he was doing.

He pushed his tongue into her mouth. It wasn't unpleasant. Actually, it was kind of nice. Then she froze. What if he touched her fangs? She struggled to end the kiss.

"Ouch, you bit me." He pulled back, touching the side of his tongue.

A soft giggle came from behind a stack of crates.

She stumbled backward, her breath leaving her body as if she'd been punched. She was a fool. This had all been a game. Clarabelle's revenge.

He gazed at her, his eyes cloudy and a bit unfocused. She had to get out of here. She moved around him and started down the path.

"Where are you going? It didn't hurt that bad." He asked, clearly shocked.

"Home," she snapped.

He caught up to her and grabbed her arm, turning her around. "It's okay. I'll teach you how to kiss."

"Clarabelle, you can come out now. I heard you." She

pulled free from his grasp, crossing her arms over her chest.

His mouth dropped open and then he glanced away, unable to meet her eyes. He knew. It was written all over his face. Her chest ached. He hadn't meant any of it.

"Don't be such a baby." Clarabelle stepped out from behind some crates.

Trinity gritted her teeth, hurt churning into anger. She would not yank out the other girl's hair and she would definitely not claw the smirk off Clarabelle's face. She would not. "I'm leaving."

"Don't," said Randy.

She wasn't sure if he was talking to her or Clarabelle.

"I was only thinking of you," Clarabelle said. "I felt bad because no one wanted to mate with you. So, I told Randy that if he wanted me, he'd have to practice on you."

Her face heated. Was she really that desperate? Obviously, she was. Tears welled in her eyes, but she wouldn't give them the satisfaction. She turned and ran away.

"Trinity, wait," Randy yelled. "It wasn't like that."

Footsteps behind her made her move faster and then there was a waft of air at her back. He was going to grab her. She could sense it. She spun around and before she could think twice she caught his arm, letting her claws come out just enough to leave hair-thin slices though his skin.

He pulled free from her grasp. "You cut me!"

"And I'll do it again, if you come any closer." She ran the rest of the way home and stopped at the front door of her hut, resting her head against the wood. Tears ran down her face, hot in the cool night air. All she wanted was a relationship like her parents had, like Troy and Remy had. Was it too much to ask for someone who she could love and who would love her too? Obviously, it was for a freak like her. She straightened, wiping the tears off her cheeks. She had to get control of herself before she saw her parents. She could not handle questions right now. She took a deep breath and opened the door.

The kitchen was empty. There was a bowl of stew on the table and some bread. She stepped inside. Harsh whispering was coming from Mom and Dad's room. They were fighting again. She was her mom's last child and Mom was sure that something bad happened to them when they were taken. Of course, Dad was positive that the teenagers were moved to another camp.

She sat at the table and took a bite of the vegetable stew. It burnt a path down her throat. Clarabelle had crossed the line this time. She pushed the dish away and walked into her bedroom, shutting the door. She flopped on her bed. How was she going to show her face around camp? She'd kissed Randy and she'd cut him. Clarabelle would not keep quiet about what had happened tonight. She didn't want to hide in her house for the next couple of weeks. She sat up. She didn't have to. She could escape into the forest and track down the previous year's Harvest Listers.

She and Travis had started sneaking out of the camp and searching the woods over three years ago, after the Almightys had taken their baby brothers for a Special List. Since everything needed water, they'd followed the Elavital River through the forest. At some point, they'd given up, but the other month when she was wandering through the brush she'd discovered that the river forked and headed back toward her encampment. She'd climbed a tree and she'd seen smoke not too far in the distance. It might have been Guards or Almightys hunting, but it could have been the other camp. It was close to home. It should only take a couple of days, a week at the most, to find out if it was another encampment.

She stood. She refused to spend her last days at home hiding in her house. She wrote a note for her parents, explaining what she was going to do and that she'd be back in a week, and placed it on her bed. She washed, changed her clothes and packed her backpack with everything she might need for a couple of days in the woods: extra clothes, water, a blanket, rope and some food. She slung the backpack over one shoulder and slipped out the back door.

She walked to the corner of the cabin, staying in the shadows. The perimeter of the camp had brick columns with fires burning every fifty to seventy-five feet, but that wasn't a problem. Producers' night vision was so poor that these were only for show, to make everyone feel safe. It was the automatic light installed by the Almightys that she had to avoid. It lit up the area like daylight. She stopped on the side of her house nearest the fence, waiting until the light passed. The Lead Producers on guard focused mainly on the forest not inside the camp but she wasn't taking any chances. The light was getting closer. A few more minutes and she could make one quick dash and be in Troy's section. By now, he'd be too busy with Remy to be actually working.

The light moved steadily from one section to another in a precise, automated glide. The sounds from the forest fell silent only to come alive as darkness once again took over. When it had passed the house, she waited a few seconds and then darted to the fence. She stayed behind the light until she came to the opening. She crawled around a bush and dropped to her knees, shrugging off her backpack. She wriggled through the hole beneath the chain link. Then she pulled her pack under the fence and raced up the hill into the forest. The air was crisp and smelled like rain. She'd save time by cutting through the thicker brush. She adjusted the backpack on her shoulders and began walking.

The farther she went the denser it became. A rustle in the weeds made her quicken her pace. She hadn't been frightened out here in years, but she'd never been this deep in the forest so late at night. She hesitated. The vegetation loomed thick and dark in front of her. Childhood tales of the creatures that inhabited the forest raced through her mind. She took a deep breath. She had to control her imagination. She'd never seen anything bigger than a fox out here, at least not in the wild.

A drop of rain hit her head. Then another one plopped on her face. She shoved into the denser brush as the sky opened and the rain fell, pelting her like stones. She kept moving. She had to find somewhere dry to wait out the storm. There was a copse of bushes to her right, but she couldn't just crawl inside. Something else might have already made this shelter its home for the night. She picked up a large stick and poked it into the bushes. There was a slight rustle from above in the tree, but then everything fell silent. This was the best she was going to get. She ducked inside.

The ground was dry, protected by the thick brush, but she was soaked. She pulled the extra clothes and blanket out of her backpack and changed, setting the wet clothes off to the side. She was still shivering, so she wrapped herself in the blanket and huddled in a tight ball, preserving her body heat. She hugged the backpack to her chest, inhaling the lemony scent of home.

The rain pattered all around and she struggled to keep her eyes open. She had to leave as soon as the storm passed. She couldn't wait to return home and tell everyone what happened to those who were taken. The other kids would have to talk to her if they wanted to hear her stories and Producers loved stories. Once they got to know her, they'd realize that she wasn't that different from them. Not on the inside where it mattered.

Trinity awoke to birds chirping and the chatter of squirrels. She stretched, her hands hitting a branch. Her eyes flew open. Sunlight filtered through thick foliage. It was daylight! She had to get moving. She climbed out of the bushes, dragging the backpack and her wet clothes behind her. The blanket was mostly dry so she stuffed that into her sack. Her clothes were still damp. If she put them away like that everything would mold. She picked up the stick that she'd used last night and tied her shirt and pants around it to dry.

She grabbed her canteen and took a long swallow, quenching her thirst. She slid its strap over her shoulder. Her stomach rumbled. She pulled an apple from her bag. She'd have to eat and walk. She'd lost a lot of time by falling asleep.

After trudging along for what seemed like forever, she stopped, wiping the sweat off her forehead. She wasn't sure how long she'd been traveling. The sun barely penetrated this area so she had no idea what time it was. It might be faster to go back and follow the river. There was a slight rustling of leaves behind her. She slowly turned around. Nothing. She unzipped the backpack, stuck her damp clothes inside and then held the stick like a club. She waited but nothing moved. It was her imagination. That was all. She started walking again. It was all those stupid stories her parents had told her about the creatures in the exhibit that inhabited the woods, but she knew the forest. The only creatures around were the birds and squirrels. All small. All harmless. Still, she couldn't shake the feeling that she was being watched. She picked up her pace. The sooner she got out of underbrush and into the open the better.

She continued moving as fast as the terrain would allow. Time seemed to lengthen. She could almost believe that she'd been traveling through this brush for days. She stumbled along, sweat dripping down her back. There was a quiet snap above her head. The leaves moved slightly. Was it from the wind or something else? She strained to pick up any sound. Was that the murmur of water? She forged forward, tearing the flesh on her arms as she shoved through thorns. She had to get out of the underbrush before she went mad. The sunlight shone through the branches. The river was up ahead. She should wait to make sure that no one was around. Guards and Almightys sometimes hunted out here, but she couldn't stop her feet from racing for the river. She burst into the clearing, glad to be free, in the open where her imagination wouldn't run so wild.

She took a long drink of water, enjoying the cool breeze on her face. By the position of the sun, it was near noon. It was earlier than she'd thought. She continued following the river. It grew larger and stronger, the rushing of the water drowning out every other sound. She stilled. That wasn't right. The river was not that loud. The forest had quieted. No chirp or chatter, only the water and the wind through the trees. The hair on her neck stood on end. Had something really been watching her in the brush and was it still following her? She moved cautiously, all senses on alert. A leaf fell and she jumped, holding the stick in front of her as a weapon. Nothing moved. The sunlight shone in her eyes, so she shaded them with her free hand. Was there something in the branches or just a shadow? If it was a creature, she shouldn't be standing there waiting for it to pounce. She slowly backed away. It was time to travel a little closer to the water.

She waited at the edge where the forest ended and the river began. The trees thinned; they were no match for the rocky land forged by the rushing water. The river itself was wide and blue. Everything looked normal. She cautiously stepped into the clearing. If something was stalking her from the forest, it would have to come out in the open. She could always run into the water. She didn't want to get wet, but she knew how to swim.

It was a harder trip on the uneven ground and the day dragged on. The sun's strong rays blinded her as she walked and her feet ached. Her stomach rumbled. She'd eat when she stopped for the night. Hunger was nothing new to her. She shifted the backpack on her shoulders and trudged around a bend. A flash caught her eye. Something silver glistened on the rocks, sparkling like ice crystals in the sunshine. It was partially submerged in the water. She cautiously approached, ready to run into the forest at any sign of danger. It was similar to her in size and shape except instead of feet and hands this creature had flippers and a long, thick tail. Its skin was silver-gray and scaly. It was hairless and lying on its side with its head in the water. There were four slits along its rib cage.

"Hey, are you all right?" She took a couple of steps back in case it was just sleeping.

The creature didn't move. She should just go. She didn't have time for this, but she'd never seen anything like it. She crept closer, her heart beating faster with each step. Her feet were in the water now. She was only a few feet away. She nudged it with the bottom of the stick and jumped back. It remained still, lifeless. She moved farther into the water and poked it again, harder this time. There was still no reaction. It was dead. *Poor, ugly thing*. What had happened to it? Had it drowned? It kind of looked like a fish. Maybe, it suffocated, stuck on the rocks and unable to get to the water. That would be sad, being that close to what it needed to live and unable to reach it.

She bent and peered at its face. It certainly was gross. Its large black eyes stared straight ahead. She jerked back. She could have sworn its eyes had adjusted but there were no whites just pupil so it was hard to tell. She stood still for several minutes but the creature didn't move. It must have been her imagination; it was certainly running wild today. She leaned in closer. Its mouth was wide open and filled with rows of long, sharp teeth. It smelled briny like the lake. Its lips quivered slightly and she jerked upright, stumbling backward and falling right next to it, within reach of its long arms.

She dropped the stick as she scrambled backward out of the water and sat panting on shore. It was alive. She was such an idiot to get so close. It lay half-in and half-out of the water, its head angled in an uncomfortable looking position. Was it in pain? She shook her head. What did that matter? She needed to go and this thing was not her problem. She stood and started to walk away. She sighed. If it was a bird or squirrel, even a mouse or rat, she'd help it without thinking twice. It wasn't the creature's fault that it was hairless and nasty looking and stinky.

She turned around and trudged over to it. If it were going to attack her it would have done it by now. She studied it closely. Two of the four slits on its side were moving a little. It was more of a slight tremble than an actual movement. The other two were stuck firmly together. As the side slits shivered, the creature's bottom jaw moved forward and back. It was like the face Adam, her baby brother, had made once when he'd swallowed too much bread. That was it! The creature was choking. She quickly filled her bottle from the river. A fish couldn't breathe air. She dumped the water over its head and chest.

The fish-man made a slight coughing sound. She jerked upright but forced herself to stay put. It still was not moving. She wasn't in any danger. She filled up her jug again and poured it on the creature. It made another gasping sound.

She had to get it back into the water. She wrinkled her nose and placed both hands on its torso and shoved, trying to push it into the river without going any deeper into the water herself. It was cold to the touch and heavy. She tried again but it didn't budge. Maybe, she could give it enough water so that it could get a deep breath and move itself. She filled up her bottle again, emptying the contents over the gills. She continued this for several minutes, but the creature remained still. This obviously wasn't working.

The creature raised its arm, hitting her thigh. She flew out of the water, screeching. She shivered as she stood on the shore wiping at her leg to remove the memory of its clammy touch. Then its arm flapped again landing on its neck. Her face heated in embarrassment. It hadn't been reaching for her. She straightened her shoulders, took a deep breath and tromped back into the river. No matter what, she was going to help this thing.

The hand that had landed on its neck moved in a grasping fashion. She bit her lip and cautiously lifted the flipper between the tips of her fingers and moved it out of the way. There were two slashes on the creature's neck. They looked like the ones on its side except these were clogged full of…something. She grimaced as she dug her finger into a slit, pulling out mud and gunk. The foul stench of rotten vegetation and feces seeped out from the slime. She flung it into the water. She turned her head to the side, took a deep breath and held it. She dug into the second slit. When it was cleared a sharp intake of raspy breath came from the fish-man and then another.

She frowned. It was breathing air, but that didn't make sense. Fish breathed underwater. She dumped water on the two slits that she'd cleared. The creature choked and gasped. It rolled away from her and clambered onto its knees. It seemed larger and more dangerous now that it was mobile. She scurried back to the safety of the shore. The fish-man took several deep breaths and then slowly dragged itself back into the water, disappearing under the waves.

She stared at the surface, her heart racing. There was no sign of it. The river flowed without a ripple of disturbance aside from the motion of the water itself. The fish-man was gone. She smiled and began to walk again, her step a little lighter. She had saved its life. She glanced warily back at the water. She and Travis used to play in the river. She wouldn't be doing that again. If there were one of those things in there, there were more.

There was a slight rustle in the brush to her left. She jumped, turning to face the forest when a splash from the river drew her gaze. A flipper dipped under the water. Her shoulders sagged. *Great. Now, I'm being hunted by land and sea.* She moved a little away from the river but not too close to the forest. It was the best that she could do.

She continued on for another hour without a sound from the river or forest, which was encouraging. It was getting late. She was going to have to find somewhere to camp for the night. She shaded her eyes from the setting sun and groaned. She was an idiot. She'd been heading west. She should have been heading east. She must have gotten turned around in the thick underbrush. She started back the way she'd come. All this time had been wasted. An entire day was gone.

A mournful howling broke the silence of the forest. A shiver danced down her spine, raising the hair on her back. A cacophony of screeches and chirps echoed from the brush. Then there was silence, not a chirp or rustle to be heard. She swallowed around a lump in her throat. Whatever made that sound was close.

There was no movement or eyes shining back at her from the brush. She hurried along. A sharp yell pierced the air. She stumbled to a halt, tipping her head to better catch the sound. There was another shout. *Guards on scent.* Had the Almightys discovered her escape? No, that was impossible. It was probably just some Guards out hunting, but that didn't solve her problem. If she were caught, she would be in deep trouble.

She had to get out of there, but which way? To her left was the river. She swallowed. She hadn't seen the fish-man for a while, but it didn't mean he wasn't lurking nearby. To her right were the woods. If something were following her, it was hiding in there. She glanced back and forth, undecided. The Guards might scare away the forest predator. She bolted into the trees. There was no way she was going to outrun them, so she had to hide.

She ran blindly away from the sound of the Guards, her backpack slamming against her spine with each stride. *If they catch my scent, they will find me*. She skidded to a stop. The forest had ended. A rock wall loomed in front of her, stretching to both sides as far as she could see. Little crevices and divots peppered the wall, but it was too steep to climb. She had to make a choice. The wrong one would cost her freedom, maybe her life.

The trees rustled behind her. *Too late. They found me*. This had all been for nothing. Now, the best she could hope for was to be taken with the others. Her chest tightened. She had to make sure that her mom and Remy weren't punished because she escaped. She raised her hands to her shoulders and slowly turned. Her breath caught in her throat. A Tracker, the deadliest of predators, stood on its back two legs, towering above her, front legs hanging down like arms. Brindle fur covered its body and its eyes glowed yellow in the shadowed forest. Its tongue lolled out the side of its mouth, exposing a row of sharp teeth on the other side. *Someone should tell it that they no longer exist in the wild.*

If you like the story, you can find it online (FREE for a limited time). Links to all stores are on my website:

http://www.lsodea.com

Or Go To

Amazon:

http://myBook.to/LOS_Escape

All Other Ebook Retailers

https://books2read.com/u/4Xgn21

ABOUT THE AUTHOR

L. S. O'Dea sees things a bit differently than most people. This is probably a by-product of being the youngest of seven children in a time when TV was only worth watching in the evenings or Saturday mornings and there were no computers. Back then, kids had to amuse themselves and being five years younger than her closest sibling she was often the unwilling entertainment.

Since she was so much younger than her brothers and sisters, it was only reasonable that they knew how to do many things that she could not, such as read and write. One day, before she started kindergarten, she really wanted to learn how to spell her name. Her mother was busy cooking or cleaning (she had seven children to care for), so her brothers were instructed to help their baby sister.

After she learned how to spell her first and middle name (Linda Sue), she raced into the kitchen to share this new knowledge with her mother. She was so proud, standing tall and reciting the letters of her name. L-E-M-O-N H-E-A-D.

Her mother was not happy with her brothers and stopped what she was doing to teach Linda the correct way to spell her name. L. S. still receives a box of Lemonhead candy every year for Christmas.

43661199R00085

Made in the USA
Lexington, KY
01 July 2019